DATE DUE			
1/8/19			
2/6/19			

Sherlock Holmes and the Seven Deadly Sins Murders

Center Point
Large Print

Also by Barry Day and available from
Center Point Large Print:

*Sherlock Holmes and the
    Shakespeare Globe Murders*
*Sherlock Holmes and the
    Alice in Wonderland Murders*
*Sherlock Holmes and the
    Copycat Murders*
*Sherlock Holmes and the
    Apocalypse Murders*

SHERLOCK HOLMES
and the
SEVEN DEADLY SINS MURDERS

BARRY DAY

CENTER POINT LARGE PRINT
THORNDIKE, MAINE

This Center Point Large Print edition
is published in the year 2017 by arrangement with
MysteriousPress.com/Open Road Integrated Media.

The text of this Large Print edition is unabridged.
In other aspects, this book may vary
from the original edition.
Printed in the United States of America
on permanent paper.
Set in 16-point Times New Roman type.

ISBN: 978-1-68324-506-3

Library of Congress Cataloging-in-Publication Data

Names: Day, Barry, author.
Title: Sherlock Holmes and the seven deadly sins murders / Barry Day.
Description: Center Point Large Print edition. | Thorndike, Maine :
Center Point Large Print, 2017.
Identifiers: LCCN 2017024366 | ISBN 9781683245063
    (hardcover : alk. paper)
Subjects: LCSH: Holmes, Sherlock—Fiction. | Watson, John H.
(Fictitious character)—Fiction. | Private investigators—England—
Fiction. | Murder—Investigation—Fiction. | Large type books. | GSAFD:
Mystery fiction.
Classification: LCC PR6054.A928 S5447 2017 | DDC 823/.914—dc23
LC record available at https://lccn.loc.gov/2017024366

34508
9|17
$37.95

For LYNNE and SONNY
. . . who both see *and* observe

CHAPTER ONE

Deuced fine looking woman, Holmes. Table by the window. Sitting with the dark fellow. Don't look now—she'll notice . . ."

"My dear Watson, if you don't think she's observed your interest from the moment we sat down, I shall have to revise my opinion of you drastically. I've always hailed your reputation with the fair sex in—what was it?—three continents . . . three and a *half,* if we are to count the sub-continent of India. But really, my dear chap, when a man sits peering covertly into the mirror and stroking his moustache every other second, what is a lady—or indeed, anyone else—to think? He is either excessively narcissistic or he is preening for the benefit of the female of the species. And since I have observed no other woman under the age of sixty in this dining room, I think it only fair to deduce that she has assumed herself to be the object of your admiration."

"So you *have* noticed her?" I detected a tiny note of triumph in my voice. I had occasionally noticed in the past that Holmes was not entirely immune to the charms of the fairer sex, even though he was inclined to view them as exhibits in some art gallery.

"It would be perverse not to, my dear

fellow, since she does indeed stand out from the somewhat windblown local flora of this benighted spot to which you have insisted on dragging me.

"But now that you insist on engaging my attention in this way, when I was perfectly happy enjoying this rather fine grouse, tell me—what do you deduce about her?"

His question gave me an excuse to take another sidelong look in the mirror that dominated one whole end of the oak beamed dining room.

The lady in question sat with her back to it and thus I could see her from both aspects. She was clearly of above average height and her fashionable evening dress of emerald silk showed off an excellent figure to advantage. Clearly patrician by the proud way she held herself and looked around her. The face an almost perfect oval with delicate, sharply defined features and a mass of ebony hair swept back from her face and pinned back with what looked like a silver comb of some sort. The fingers that toyed with her wine glass were long and slender and—for some reason I was glad to see—free of artificial colouring.

Whenever I chance to see an attractive woman in recent years, I find myself wondering what my dear late wife, Mary, would have said about her. Somehow I felt she would have approved—not simply of the woman's elegance but of something about her expression. Despite being the possessor of singular beauty, she appeared to my eye to be vulnerable and a little . . . lost.

I became aware that Holmes was looking at me with the hint of a smile at the corner of his mouth. He was still waiting for me to answer his question.

"Hm. Certainly not from these islands with an olive complexion like that. Southern European— probably Italian or Spanish. Possibly an aristocrat. The jewels certainly denote wealth . . ." The lady was now playing nervously with a necklace that would have swallowed up my Army pension several times over.

"Couturier dress—Paris or Milan at a guess . . ." Mary would almost certainly have been able to name the designer. "Here on vacation and beginning to regret it. Wishes she could exchange the so-called Scottish mist for the sun of her native clime," I concluded triumphantly, pleased at that poetic touch. "How did I do?"

"Excellent, my dear chap, excellent. Your observation about the weather was absolutely correct. Our friendly innkeeper informs me that we may expect several days of uninterrupted rain—reason enough, I fancy, for us to bring forward the date of our return to the wilds of Baker Street to—shall we say?—tomorrow morning.

"Other than that, I believe you have missed every other point of significance. As you say, the lady is certainly not from these parts but her colouring is not the olive complexion of one of the Mediterranean countries. Together with the distinctive facial contours, particularly around the eyes and forehead, that face suggests the very far north of India—perhaps even Tibet—where the racial characteristics of many races have fused over the centuries.

"Then there is the perfume she is wearing . . ."

Holmes laughed outright at my expression of surprise.

"Oh, yes. One could hardly fail to notice it as she passed our table when she entered the room. I have, as you know, Watson, made some small study of perfumes and flatter myself that I can distinguish seventy-five individual fragrances. Her own is a compound of jasmine and certain other essences exclusive to that part of the world. In my observation women tend to use a favourite perfume to define themselves. Once they have adopted it, so to speak, they almost forget they are wearing it. It is the same with a man and his choice of tobacco. You, for instance, carry with you the unmistakable hint of your beloved Arcadia mixture . . ."

I refrained from commenting on his own person in that regard, though there have been occasions—particularly in the early mornings after a three pipe problem had been involved—when I might well have done so.

"Furthermore," he continued, "the comb she is wearing in her hair confirms my analysis. Although I cannot see it clearly at this distance, I would wager it is of silver filigree in the shape of . . ." He took another careful look in the mirror as the woman turned her head to address her companion. "Most interesting—in the shape of entwined serpents. Now, where have I seen that design . . . ? If only I had my trusty Index with me! However . . . as for the dress, Maximilian in the Rue St. Honoré unless I miss my guess . . ."

Then, seeing my evident surprise—"You see, Watson, I do occasionally allow my perusal of the daily press to go beyond the police news and the agony columns. But to be fair, old fellow, there was an article about the work of that particular designer a few days ago and a photograph of that particular dress with, I am reasonably sure, that very lady wearing it. And by the *way* she wears it, she is no stranger to expensive European clothes. Consequently, I deduce that she has lived in Europe for some time and is currently concerned at the prospect of leaving it against her will . . ."

"But how can you possibly tell that, Holmes? The rest I grant you. After the time I spent in India, I should have spotted the other things for myself. But as you are so fond of saying—I see but I do not observe . . ."

"What you do not observe, being taken as you are by the lady's physical appearance, is her body language. She is restless to the point of being anxious about something. We have established that it is not because she feels she is wearing false feathers. She is used to them and she knows they become her. Therefore, she is concerned about her companion—who is clearly a compatriot—and what he is telling her. She most emphatically does not want to hear it."

His words caused me to focus my attention properly for the first time on the lady's companion. He was a small, compact little man, also wearing western dress but, unlike her, he seemed ill at ease in it and from time to time would run his finger around the inside of his collar, as though he found it constricting. His complexion was significantly swarthier than her own and, although his back was to me, I could see from his reflection in the mirror that a pair of bright little eyes were fixed hypnotically on her. And while his manner in general seemed respectful to the point of being deferential, he was clearly being insistent about something or other to the lady's obvious discomfort. Every so often those splendid eyes of hers would flash and her body would tense in disagreement. They were not a happy couple. In fact, I would have been prepared to bet that they were not a couple at all in any true sense of the word. Even if she were not there under actual duress, the Emerald Lady—as I was beginning to think of her—was certainly not there by choice. I would have given a great deal to have overheard what she was arguing so vehemently with him about.

That, however, was not to be . . .

Before I go any further I should explain what Holmes and I were doing in a small and perfectly charming hotel in the heart of Scotland.

An old Army chum of mine had decided to rent a shoot for a few days around the "Glorious 12th" and invited a few of us up to join him for what promised to be a convivial occasion. Much as I was tempted by the offer, I was concerned about leaving Holmes on his own in Baker Street.

It was only some six months since the Jack the Ripper affair and I think the full significance of what we had been involved in had struck us both as a delayed reaction. Being, if I do say so myself, of a more resilient temperament, I was now able to see the whole business in some sort of perspective and got back into my old routine. Holmes, on the other hand, was inclined to brood and, now that the danger was safely past, had sunk into something of a depression.

After much persuasion on my part—and more to please me, I suspect, than anything else—he had agreed to accompany me.

"Well, Watson," he said, "the trip will at least allow me to solve one mystery."

"And what is that, pray?"

"Just how good a shot you are, old fellow! I must confess that, although I always insist on your bringing your service revolver along on these various jaunts of ours, I have never been entirely confident of your aim, particularly when I myself was in the immediate vicinity of your supposed target."

So pleased was I that he would accompany me that I let him have his little joke. There were a few Afghan tribesmen (now deceased) who could testify to the eye of John H. Watson, M.D., late of the 5th Northumberland Fusiliers.

To be fair, once Holmes had decided to play a part, he played it well and thoroughly enjoyed his own performance, for a while at least. My old colleagues, who knew him mostly by repute as something of a recluse, were positively charmed by his manner and duly impressed by his knowledge of the most arcane aspects of hunting game.

"My dear Holmes," I had cause to say to him on more than one occasion, "I had no idea you knew so much about the subject!"

"Nor did I," he replied laconically, "until I decided that, having committed myself to this fool's errand—no offence, my dear fellow!—I would master the theory of the subject first. Frankly, I must admit I found the intellectual exercise involved reasonably stimulating."

On the first day of the shoot he consented

to come out with us, bagged a couple of fine specimens with his first two shots, then, muttering that he failed to see the challenge, retired to the lodge to read some dry tome or other.

When, earlier in the day, the weather changed for the worse and the locals shook their heads as one and claimed that the rain had set in for the duration, I made the excuse of pressing business back in London. Honour having been served all round and Holmes having had the enforced rest that I, as his medical man, adjudged he needed, we took ourselves off to the greater comfort of the local inn. Tomorrow we were to take the train back to London and pick up the threads.

Holmes, I could tell, was like a racehorse champing at the bit. The countryside held little charm for him; the maze of the metropolis with its infinite possibilities was where that amazing mind could feed itself.

Over an excellent dinner he had been positively playful—for him always a good sign—even if the humour was, as so often, at my expense. But now the playfulness had dropped away and I could tell that something about the rather exotic couple had engaged his interest.

At that point two men entered the room almost simultaneously. One was Mine Host, who made way politely for the other, an undistinguished man of medium height, who made straight for the Emerald Lady's table and engaged the two of them in animated conversation without even taking a seat.

I freely admit that, had I possessed lip reading skills, I would have eavesdropped on what they were saying. For some unaccountable reason the whole party had captured my interest. It was as though I had walked into some play and wanted to see what happened next, even though I had no idea of the plot.

Nor was I destined to find out, for at that very moment the landlord was hovering at our table and apologising for interrupting our meal.

"I trust everything was to your satisfaction, Mr. Holmes . . . Dr. Watson? We try our best but in these out of the way spots . . ."

"And you succeed admirably." Holmes was at his most courteous. "Dr. Watson and I were just saying that the grouse were cooked to perfection . . ."

"Absolute perfection," I chipped in.

"Ah, well, sir, it always helps in the kitchen if they're not full of yon pellets. You're a remarkable clean shot, Mr. Holmes."

"These were the birds *you* shot, Holmes?"

"I felt I should make some small contribution to the festivities, my dear fellow, and when I saw the carnage you and your friends were inflicting, I took the precaution . . . But I don't believe the wellbeing of our birds was the only business you had with us, landlord? Didn't I notice the local constabulary hovering without?"

"Indeed you did, Mr. Holmes. Sergeant Drummond was wondering if he could have a word?"

"Indeed, he may," my friend replied, bunching his napkin and rising from the table. "If you will excuse me for a moment, Watson. It will enable you to pursue your ornithological researches uninterrupted." He nodded his head imperceptibly in the direction of the other table as he followed the landlord to the doorway, where I could see a sturdy fellow in uniform. It seemed to me that he was looking distinctly uncomfortable. It was an expression I had often seen on the faces of those meeting Mr. Sherlock Holmes for the first time.

Swirling the last mouthful of an excellent Beaune around in the bottom of my glass, I held it up to the light, pretending to examine it but, in reality, giving me the opportunity to glance across at the table opposite.

The newcomer had now drawn up a chair and the three of them were conversing in angry whispers. Several times the Emerald Lady shook her head angrily and appeared increasingly distressed, though her native companion remained impassive. Now the white man was obviously indicating the policeman conversing with Holmes beyond the glass door that enclosed the dining room, although he did so with minimal movement of his head, so as not to be obvious.

Perhaps I took a little too long to admire so little wine, for the dark fellow looked in my direction and said something warningly to the others. It was clear that they were now aware of both my presence and my interest. There was a scrape of chairs on the stone floor and the group swept past me and out of the room. I saw Holmes and the sergeant move aside to give them room but the courtesy went unacknowledged.

As they passed me, I thought I'd take a leaf from Holmes's book. See *and* observe. The Emerald Lady I knew I'd recognise anywhere. Her compatriot, too. Ferrety little fellow you wouldn't want to meet on a dark night. The third man? Harder to pin down. Middle-aged, blondish, bland sort of public schoolboyish face that would probably look very much the same at seventy as it had at seventeen. The sort of chap you could sit next to in the club for years and then not recognise when you passed him in the street.

But then, why would I need to?

While I was still collating all these impressions, I realised that Holmes was standing at my side. The look in his eyes told me that something had happened to spark his interest. The man was never so alive as when he had the scent of a problem in search of a solution.

"Come along, Watson," he said. "We can't have you sitting here daydreaming when there is work to be done. The sergeant appears to have encountered a small *crise* and would be grateful to have the opinion of Sherlock Holmes, the famous consulting detective—and, of course, his trusty friend and associate, Dr. Watson, if we weren't too busy. I took the liberty of assuring him that we could spare him a few moments in our busy schedule."

Even though I rather resented the intrusion on our privacy, it always pleased me to see Holmes so alert and cheerful. That mind was like a racing engine; it had to be harnessed or it would shake itself to pieces. And in any case, what did it matter, now that we had had our break and were ready to depart?

Nonetheless, I wasn't going to let him get off entirely scot-free. As I followed him to the door and the waiting sergeant, I grumbled—"What is it? Some drunken crofter fallen over a sheep, I suppose?"

"Nothing so exciting, I'm afraid, old fellow. It seems that one of the local gentry has been found dead—in a locked room. Who knows, perhaps you will find a place for it in one of your little narratives . . ."

CHAPTER TWO

Sorry to interrupt your dinners, gentlemen. I know Harry here puts on a fair spread but we'd really welcome your assistance on a wee matter that's just now occurred up at the big house. We're used to a little poaching, maybe someone borrowing a bicycle now and then, so we're a wee bit out of our depth, I fear, with this happening. We'd be most grateful if you could take a look and give us your opinion, Mr. Holmes."

And, in truth, Sergeant Drummond did look a "wee bit" out of his depth for the rain that had been beating down ceaselessly for the past two days had left him bedraggled and looking somewhat forlorn. However, as his carriage bowled along the narrow country roads, he cheered up considerably, now that he had someone to share his burden, and began to tell us his story.

"Aye, Mr. Holmes—Doctor—it's to the big house I'm taking you, for it's there it happened. We called it The Manse in the old days but when the Briggs fellow moved in—him with his English Southern ways—he insisted on calling it The Hall. Behaved like a Southern gentleman, too, he did. He was 'Sir' down there, so he wanted us all to call him one up here . . ." Then

21

his craggy face allowed itself a small grin. "But we're awful forgetful in these parts."

"I take it, Sir—"

"Simon."

"I take it Sir Simon isn't too popular with his neighbours, then?" I asked.

"*Wasn't,* Doctor—*wasn't*. You see the poor man's dead. And nobody wished that upon him."

Then, seeing my surprise, he went on—

"See, he came here about a couple of years ago now. Made his money in London, so they said, then decided to retire and become a Lord of the Manor. Picked the wrong spot, as I say, but that's beside the point. He bought the big house, did it up, money no object. Then, when he found his London ways didna go down so well hereaboots, he started to keep hisself to hisself. He had his staff to look after everything. You wouldna see him from one month to the next.

"Then, a few days ago, he comes storming into my police station, bangs the counter and says he's being spied on and he won't have it. He pays his taxes—which is more than many around here do—and he wants it stopped. Well, I can tell you—I was fair taken aback. He wasn't a popular man, that's for certain, but I couldna believe anyone meant him any harm."

"Had he seen any of the people who were spying?" asked Holmes from the dim depths of the jolting carriage.

"Aye, now there's the even queerer thing," Drummond replied, turning in his direction. "He claimed they were clever at hiding themselves but not quite clever enough. There were two of them and he'd caught a glimpse of them one night when he was watching and the moon suddenly came out from behind a cloud. One of them was an average looking sort of fellow . . ."

"And the other was an Indian?"

The sergeant peered even harder into the gloom that engulfed Holmes.

"Why, yes, Mr. Holmes, that's just what he claimed. But how do you know? And what does it mean?"

"Possibly nothing. But I see the lights of what I presume to be the big house approaching. Perhaps you will be good enough to tell us how Sir Simon died, for I presume it is *his* death we are here to investigate?"

"Indeed, it is. Indeed, it is. His butler, Blackmore, came to the station in a fearful state with the news. But here we are. He'll best tell you about it hisself . . ."

The carriage had been rattling along a curved driveway and now came to a stop in front of what I suppose was an imposing granite house, though the driving rain made it difficult to discern the details and did nothing to relieve the air of gloom that surrounded it and which certainly extended to the gaunt figure of the man who had the door already open for us.

Blackmore was a tall, cadaverous man in his sixties. I learned later that Sir Simon had brought him up from a London agency and at this moment—and, I suspect, for some time past—the man was regretting the move north of the border. At the moment he was clearly shaken and it is at times like this that Holmes comes into his own.

We were in a kind of baronial hall that led off into a series of other rooms and the place was clearly a rambling mausoleum distinctly lacking in charm of any sort. Briggs had imported his idea of traditional British aristocratic splendour of decor and dropped it piecemeal into a setting it ill fitted. I sensed that in many ways it was symbolic of the man's failure to fit into his new environment.

Taking Blackmore gently by the arm, my friend led him to an armchair and sat him down, slightly apart from the sergeant and myself. Then, speaking very quietly, he said—

"Now then, Mr. Blackmore, I'd like you to tell me in your own words what happened here this evening. Omit no detail, however trivial, for it may be of the greatest importance."

Holmes's tone clearly had the desired effect, for in a moment the story came pouring forth.

"The Master's been worried sick for days,

sir," he said—forgetting in his distress his professional accent and lapsing into what must have been his native Cockney. "What with these people watching the house. Oh, yes, I've seen them with me own eyes and it's my opinion as how they *wanted* to be seen, wanted 'im to *know* they had their eye on him, like.

"When I told 'im I'd seen them too, the Master just looked at me and said—'Blackmore,' he said, 'looking is *all* they'll do. I'll get the law on them, you see if I don't. I've worked too 'ard for what I've got and no common burglars are going to take it from me.'"

"So that's what he thought they were—common burglars?" This from Sergeant Drummond. Seeing that Blackmore was calmer now the floodgates had been breached, the sergeant and I had edged closer.

"What else could they be? We keep ourselves to ourselves here, we do. It's no secret the Master's got—had—a bob or two. Stands to reason. Wouldn't be a 'Sir' and all otherwise, would he?"

An interesting social commentary, I thought.

"And then he's got all these valuable collections from his travels. Coins, pottery, books and that. Course, he doesn't just leave them lying around. Keeps—kept—the really good stuff in that special room he had built in the Library. And that's where . . ."

For a moment the memory seemed about to

overwhelm him but he continued as he pulled himself to his feet.

"I'd best show you, gentlemen. That's what you're here for, after all . . ."

He led the way to one of the side rooms and we found ourselves in what was obviously the formal Library. Expensive armchairs, fussy little side tables to go with them and the walls lined with book shelves on which the books appeared to be arranged in order of size and the colour of their bindings. It was some interior designer's idea of what a club library should look like and somehow it failed in its effect, like the rest of the house. It was a self-conscious act of creation rather than the expression of an individual personality.

Blackmore was now leading us towards another closed door in the middle of one wall.

"When we moved in, the Master had this built special. Brought workmen in from down South, so that the locals wouldn't know nothing about it . . ." Stress was doing nothing for the butler's grammar. "Completely airtight, he said it was. 'Just the right temperature, Blackmore, so that nothing will spoil. Don't want this damned climate . . .'" and he cast an apologetic glance at Drummond—"'rotting the family fortunes, do we?' He was joking, like, but he meant it, too.

"Then this evening he seemed particularly nervy. For days now he'd been most insistent that when it started to get dark, I should do my rounds and check all the locks on the doors and windows. Tonight he made me do it all over again. Then he said he'd have his supper in the Library—just something on a tray—and he didn't want to be disturbed. When I'd brought it in and left it on that table there . . ." He indicated one of the small tables, where a brass tray with a plate of sandwiches and an opened half bottle of hock and wine glass stood, apparently untouched. ". . . then I heard him lock the door behind me.

"And that's the last time I saw the Master alive."

"And then what happened?" Holmes asked quietly.

"I went about my duties as per usual and about a couple of hours later I happened to be passing the Library. No, I tell a lie . . ."—he shot a defiant look at Holmes—"I made it my business to pass the Library more than I strictly needed to. I was worried about 'im, see? And at one point, about an hour or so after he'd gone in, I could have sworn I heard him talking to someone. Then it stopped and the next time I passed—nothing. So I reckoned I must have been mistaken.

"Another hour went by and then I took me courage in me hands and knocked on the door. I was going to say I'd come to clear his supper things but there was no answer and I knocked several times. That's when I started to get the wind up. I've got a spare set of keys for the whole 'ouse . . ." and he produced a large key ring chained to his belt in proof—"So I fished 'em out and opened the door . . ."

"And found?" I interjected.

"Nothing. The room was empty. Then I noticed that one of the French windows was slightly open and there were wet marks on the floor. My first thought was—'That's how the devils got in and they've kidnapped 'im!' But then . . ."

His eyes turned to the closed door in the middle of the room . . .

"Now that I came to examine it more closely, I could see that, although it was painted to look like the mahogany of the rest of the room, it was in reality made of some heavy metal and fitted flush."

In a few strides Holmes stood in front of it and turned the handle—but to no effect.

"A false face and a dead hand. A most interesting combination. This, I take it, is your master's *chambre privé*?"

"That's right, sir. His inner sanctum, he called it. And that's what killed 'im. I thought it best to put it back just the way I found it. Let me show you but, if you don't mind, I don't think I'm up to going in there again."

Blackmore moved over to the door and removed a small picture that hung next to it. Behind it was a control panel not so very different from that for a normal electric light, except that this one had buttons and dials instead of switches.

The butler indicated without touching a black button.

"This is what opens the door. This . . ."—he pointed to a red button—". . . is the master lock that over-rides everything else . . . and *this* . . ." here he indicated a large metal dial—"this changes the air in the room to keep it fresh . . ."

Seeing my puzzled expression, Holmes interrupted.

"This, my dear Watson, is the very recent invention of a leading Swiss banking company. Its primary purpose—apart from providing literally cast iron security—is to keep the air in the chamber at a controlled temperature and humidity, in order to protect important documents from deteriorating. However, I very much fear that that purpose has been subverted on this occasion.

"You see this vent . . . ?" He indicated a solid looking metal mesh about six inches square. "Its purpose is to allow the air in the room to be recycled at intervals. To that end it has built into it a fan that will efficiently remove the stale air from the room and replace it with a suitably filtered fresh supply. On this occasion, however, the delicate controls have been deliberately tampered with, leaving—I would suspect—the chamber a perfect vacuum."

"And Nature abhors a vacuum," I said. I'm not sure why. The line just came into my head.

"Indeed, it does, Watson. And I very much fear that Sir Simon came to share that dislike with Spinoza."

As he spoke, Holmes was operating the controls with those long thin fingers, as if he had actually invented the infernal machine.

Suddenly there was a metallic click and the "door" swung open. Crouched on the floor, almost in an attitude of prayer was the figure of a middle-aged man.

I heard Drummond behind me say in a frightened tone—"Aye, that's Sir Simon, right enough. Poor man!" And then Holmes . . .

"Your department, I think, Watson?"

It took me no time to reach the body, for there was no doubt that was what we were dealing with and my search for any sign of a pulse was hardly necessary. If I had not heard the explanation and seen the locale for myself, I should easily have concluded that the man had died of asphyxiation. The face had that distinctive blue-ish tinge but it was the eyes that held you. They protruded and in them I swear one could see the horror that was passing through the victim's mind in those last few agonising seconds, when he realised that he was to die in a trap of his own making, as the last of the air was sucked out of the chamber.

No bonds, no gags had been necessary. Just

God's natural elements or, in this case, the lack of them.

As I was pondering this irony and checking to see that there were no other telltale cuts or abrasions—there were not—I heard Blackmore say—

"That would account for that funny noise, sir, when I opened the vault. A sort of rushing noise, like air coming in. I thought it might be from the window, like, but then I'd already pushed that to."

"Correct. It was the air in the room filling up the vacuum," said Holmes. "Now, Watson, I believe Sir Simon has told us all he has to tell. What do we deduce from the context?"

I closed the poor devil's eyes and straightened up to look around me.

"It's pretty obvious that whoever did this came in by that window. Even locked, it wouldn't take much forcing for a determined man . . ."

"And I think we may take it that our friends were most certainly that," said Holmes, who was by now over by the window in question.

"Three people entered this room through this window and left the way they came. As Dr. Watson rightly points out, the lock has been forced with a sharp instrument, probably a knife point. The heavy rain makes three sets of footprints clearly visible on entering, less so when they leave.

"Two of them are men—one of middle height, one of them possibly slightly less. The taller man's prints are greatly blurred over by the vault, probably because he was struggling with Briggs . . ."

"And the third?" I asked and was surprised to see Holmes wore that opaque expression, which is his way of telling me not to pursue a line of questioning in public.

"That is not immediately clear to me."

Then, moving back into the centre of the room—

"And what do we suppose happened then?"

"I should have thought that was pretty clear, Mr. Holmes." This from Drummond. "They subdued their victim, while they ransacked the place for the valuables."

"I think not, Sergeant. Certainly, they restrained Sir Simon, so that he could not interfere, but they were not looking for 'valuables' in the plural. This room is full of portable objects that your common or garden burglar would stuff his pockets with—objects that are easily disposed of. And yet, Sergeant, I would be prepared to wager the contents of this room against your pension that an inventory will show nothing is missing."

As he spoke, we all found ourselves looking round the Library and through the open door to the vault beyond. Clearly, objects had been moved, drawers and cupboards left open, but there was no sign of vandalism such as is normally to be found at the scene of a robbery.

"Precisely. These people came here in search of one thing and did not find it. They thrust Sir Simon into the vault, then left. But one of them came back, because he had a further mission to fulfil—he came to kill Sir Simon . . ."

"But, Holmes, how can you possibly know that?"

"The footprints tell their own story, old fellow, thanks to the rain. One set—and one set only—is still wet, which indicates that they were made later than the rest. There is one other thing . . ."

"Chloroform!" I cried. "I caught a faint whiff of it when I examined the body but I was so taken with the look of the fellow . . ."

"And it was, indeed, now very faint. In fact, if the vault had not been completely airless, I doubt if such a volatile substance would still have been detectable at all. No, my guess is that Sir Simon was interrogated to no avail, then rendered unconscious while the intruders searched for what they had come to find. Failing in that search, they departed empty handed.

"Then . . . one of their number returned the way he had come on some pretext, bundled the still unconscious man into the vault and sealed it, effectively condemning its occupant to death. Before he did so, he left two small messages for us to find . . ."

"Messages?" said Drummond. "I didna see any notes left lying aroond. Did you, Blackmore?"

"Because there were none to find, gentlemen. No piece of paper saying—'I confess to the murder of Sir Simon Briggs. Signed X.' But there were messages, nonetheless, if we can only decipher them.

"Two, to be precise. This is one . . ."

He turned to the body and gently brushed the hair back from the forehead. There, roughly marked in what looked like soot from the fireplace, was a crude letter "A."

"Someone has read their Hawthorne, gentlemen. *The Scarlet Letter*. If I recall, the heroine was marked by having a letter emblazoned on her forehead, so that the world should know what she was. Our murderer clearly wants us to know what he, at least, believes his victim to be. Something that begins with 'A'."

"You said there were *two* messages, Holmes."

"Ah, yes. The second is by your elbow, Watson, on that occasional table. The framed photograph. Perhaps you will be good enough . . . ?"

It was only then that I noticed among all the disarray a simple wooden frame. As I picked it up, I noticed that it appeared to be the only object that was actually damaged, for the glass had been broken.

It was a photograph of a group of young men— the kind of thing any of us might keep as a souvenir of a class or a team of which we were part in our youth. There were seven of them, standing somewhat self-consciously posed for the camera in two rows in what looked like some sort of courtyard. They looked to be all of an age—somewhere in their very early twenties—and were clearly good friends, for several of them had their arms linked.

The only distinguishing feature was that each of them—except one—was wearing a sweater with a large capital letter across the chest. But whereas in every team photo I can recall seeing, the symbols are identical, these were not.

One was wearing an "L," another a "G." Then there was an "R," a "P," an "E" and . . . an "A."

There was one other thing about the photograph that caught my eye.

"Good heavens, Holmes—the 'A' . . ."

"Quite right, old fellow, the letter 'A' has been eliminated from the alphabet—in facsimile as in real life."

Someone had crudely slashed across the face of the young man wearing the "A" on his sweater.

CHAPTER THREE

A few hours later we were in the express rattling south, the telegraph poles flickering past with hypnotic regularity. It is one of Holmes's pastimes on train journeys to time the distance between their passing and so estimate the speed with which we are travelling but today he was otherwise preoccupied.

On his knee he had the defaced photograph from Sir Simon Briggs's Library and he was studying it with the utmost concentration. When I first realised what he had there, I had raised the obvious question.

"Surely, Holmes, removing it represents tampering with evidence at the scene of a crime?"

"You are quite right, of course, Watson, but the solution of this particular crime is not to be found in the hills and glens of Bonnie Scotland. Before I left, I advised the good Sergeant Drummond to bring in Scotland Yard on the grounds that Briggs was merely a visiting Sassenach and whose history lay firmly south of the border. He breathed a sigh of relief and said he was of the same mind exactly. At this very moment it may cheer your soul to think that Lestrade's minions are even now heading to the place we have just left."

"So I take it you don't believe these were a gang of local thieves and that things somehow got out of hand?"

"Oh, yes, I certainly believe things got out of hand. The original group were clearly looking for a specific something that they did not find. Then one of them returned with his own separate and personal agenda, which—as you saw—he carried out most efficiently . . ."

"To kill Sir Simon?"

"To kill Sir Simon—or Mr. 'A,' as we may call him. Not merely *kill* him—*deface* him." And he held the photo up to the early morning light coming through the carriage window.

"The question we have to ask ourselves is—why? And the answer to that, I venture to suggest, Watson, lies in the identity and location of Messrs. 'G,' 'L,' 'P,' 'R,' and 'E.' "

"And precisely how do you propose to determine that?" I asked. "If Briggs is indeed 'A'—which I am perfectly prepared to admit—how does that help us? That photograph was certainly taken many years ago."

"It helps us because it speaks to us, old fellow. Not through the *dramatis personae* but through the location. That photograph was taken in the main quadrangle of Christ Church College, Oxford—a place I know well from the days when my brother Mycroft was an undergraduate there. I have little doubt but that he may be able to throw a ray of light that will enable us to move a step or two further. When we have removed the dust of travel from our persons, I propose that we pay him a visit and see what we can discover about these alphabetical gentlemen."

"And you believe that will lead us to Briggs's attackers?"

"Oh, I hardly think we shall have too much trouble locating them. You see, we have already seen them."

"What do you mean—*seen* them?"

At this Holmes reached into an inside pocket and extracted an envelope. From it he shook a couple of bright green threads on to the palm of his hand.

"Briggs's visitors—one of them his attacker—were undoubtedly the group dining at the inn with us last night. There can be few people in that part of the world who were wearing emerald green silk last night. I recovered these fibres from the window frame while you were examining the body. But even without their corroboration, surely you noticed the hint of the lady's perfume in the room? Even the chloroform could not entirely obscure it . . . ."

"And they had the infernal audacity to murder a man and then sit down to dinner!"

"I don't think they *did* murder him. I believe they paid their visit, found it to be fruitless and left Briggs—as they thought—subdued but unharmed. It was another of their party—almost certainly that late arrival at dinner—who doubled back and finished the job. Unless the lady and her companion were actors of the first order, they were genuinely disturbed by what he had to tell them and I would wager *that* was an expurgated version of the facts as we now know them.

"Whatever his relationship with them, he has achieved one other result . . ."

"And that is?"

"He has grappled them to his soul with hoops of steel, as Shakespeare would have it. Your lady friend may have originally committed the comparatively minor crime of being an accessory to breaking and entering but now she is involved up to her elegant ears in murder."

And with that, he tucked the photograph securely into his luggage, pulled his hat down over his eyes and said not a word until the train reached King's Cross.

Holmes has the knack of summoning up sleep at will. He can catnap anywhere and wake up completely refreshed. It's a knack I have never been able to master and, consequently, when we reached Baker Street, I would have welcomed forty winks but my contradictory friend—in contrast to his Highland lethargy—was now full of energy.

"Come along, Watson. Here we have the first

case that promises to be of the slightest interest to cross our path in months and you want to sleep. I do believe, if you had your way, you would condemn me to the pursuit of schoolgirls' lost pencil cases, so that you could put your feet up!"

I could have pointed out that a year that had involved the man in cases—quite apart from the Apocalypse business—as diverse as the sudden death of Cardinal Tosca, an inquiry he carried out at the express desire of His Holiness the Pope, and the affair of Wilson, the notorious canary trainer, which, it was generally agreed, had removed a plague spot from the East End of London, could hardly qualify as dull. But when Holmes was in this mood, there was no arguing with him. So I did not tempt providence.

Then he did say something that sparked my attention.

"Surely you want to find your Woman in Green again?"

And I had to admit to myself that, in fact, I did.

He was generous enough to permit us a cup of tea before we set off to seek Mycroft at his habitual lair, the Diogenes Club and I was just settling in my chair with mine when the door bell rang down below and I heard Mrs. Hudson admit someone. A tread on the fourteen steps that I had learned to recognise over the years, a familiar tap on the door and the equally familiar face of

Inspector Lestrade of Scotland Yard peered round it.

"Well met, Lestrade. Just the man I wanted to see," cried Holmes, slipping on his jacket as he entered the room from his bedroom. "What news from the north?"

"And good day to you, too, Mr. Holmes—Doctor," Lestrade replied, too seasoned a campaigner to be rushed. "Why, thank you, Doctor, I *will* have a cup, if you're pouring." And he took the proffered cup, which had been intended for Holmes, who gave me a glance that told me he had read the unspoken message.

"Very well, Watson, a place for everything and everything in its place. You may well be right." And he sank into his usual chair with good grace.

How often had the three of us sat here like this, I reflected, while events grave and gay, some of them affecting the highest in the land, were unfolding around us. How often had the decisions we had arrived at in this room changed the lives of hundreds, even though they were never to be aware of it?

We were an ill-assorted trio. Holmes, thin and angular, perched in his chair at a moment like this, as if ready to take flight. Lestrade, small, almost—if I'm honest—ferrety but as tenacious as any of that under-rated species when he had determined his target. And me—how did I view myself? A middle-aged ex-soldier of no particular distinction with a war wound that played up in the damp weather. And yet that remarkable man, Holmes, had told me on more than one occasion that I completed him—so who was I to argue. Certainly the three of us had survived more than a few adventures together and it seemed as though we were about to embark upon another.

"News from the north, eh?" Lestrade said at length, carefully putting down his cup and saucer on the floor beside his equally carefully-folded topcoat. He then took a piece of paper from an inside pocket.

"I received this cable from my men up there just before I came out." He smoothed it flat and began to peruse it. "They essentially confirm your analysis of the situation, Mr. 'Olmes . . ." He scanned the document for the key points.

"A dark complexioned gentleman, giving what I'm pretty sure will turn out to be a false name, rented a house in the vicinity . . . seen there with a foreign woman described as being 'very striking' . . ." A gross understatement, I found myself thinking. "Joined yesterday by another man nobody could describe too well. All of them skedaddled in the middle of the night . . . Oh, everything paid up. In fact, it was *because* they paid well over the odds in advance and no questions asked to rent the place that the locals paid so much attention to them.

"No sign of them on the train, so they must have had their own transport ready and waiting."

"Yes, yes, Lestrade," Holmes interrupted testily, "but what about the scene of the crime?"

"Very much as you said," the Inspector replied, not to be hurried in his account as he consulted the telegram. "The controls of that there vault were properly seen to. There was no way that poor devil could have got out, short of using dynamite . . ."

"Which would have blown him to Kingdom Come, anyway," I added helpfully.

"Just so, Doctor," said Lestrade, returning like for like. "Even supposing he'd happened to have any dynamite with him. The locals have got search parties out in the area but, frankly, gentlemen . . ."

"The birds have undoubtedly flown, where even Watson's friends, armed to the teeth as they are, could not reach them."

"Just so, Mr. 'Olmes," said the Inspector, clearly puzzled by the reference.

"There is just one other small matter, Lestrade," said Holmes, producing the framed photograph, which had been lying face down on the table next to his chair.

He then proceeded to explain the circumstances in which he found it.

Lestrade gave him a glance that would have rooted most men to the spot but somehow it also managed to convey that he knew it was pointless to debate the issue.

"So you believe this piece of *evidence* suggests that one or more of these other men in this here picture may have something to do with the death of Sir Simon?"

"I believe it is an assumption we must explore, Lestrade, if only to eliminate it. Sir Simon does not appear to have been exactly a modest man and there were various likenesses of him around the room, not least the life-size portrait over the fireplace, and yet in conjunction with the fact that it is the only one in which he is seen wearing the initial letter that was painted on his body—and I think the odds narrow considerably.

"Furthermore, Lestrade, if I were a betting man, I would be prepared to wager that we have a sporting chance of shortening them still further, if we consult the Oracle forthwith . . ."

In answer to Lestrade's puzzled frown, I added—"Brother Mycroft."

Holmes consulted his watch. "And by my calculation we have precisely one hour before he goes in to dinner, a ritual that is totally sacrosanct. I presume you have retained your official carriage, Lestrade . . . ?"

The Diogenes Club is unobtrusively situated in Pall Mall and for greater convenience Mycroft has rooms just opposite. Its ability to melt into the background is one of the attributes its members value most highly.

They have one other attribute in common. None of them wishes to have communication with his fellow members. The "No Talking" rule is so strictly enforced that to break it is to risk summary expulsion from an institution that has gained a reputation for having as its members the most unsociable and unclubable men in town. I remember Holmes once telling me that his brother had been one of the founding members and largely responsible for drawing up its code of conduct. I had found it an unsettling experience on the one previous occasion I had had cause to visit its dingy premises. To the best of my knowledge, Lestrade had never been within its portals and I looked forward to watching his reaction.

I cannot honestly say that Mycroft Holmes looked pleased to see our little delegation. When the porter, who bore a distinct resemblance to an undertaker in both dress and demeanour, had winkled him out of the recesses of the club, his first reaction was to check his fob watch before even a word of greeting had been exchanged.

"Do not concern yourself, brother mine, our mission is brief," said Holmes and that seemed to cheer the elder brother enough to merit a wintry smile and a flaccid shake of the hand for Lestrade and myself.

"I believe the Strangers' Room is free." It was more of a statement than a question for the porter, who nodded. "It is the only room in the club where talking is allowed," Mycroft continued rather smugly, as he led the way down a dimly-lit corridor into the bowels of the building.

Then, as if almost apologising for his lack of courtesy, he turned his bland mandarin face towards Lestrade. "You must forgive our byzantine little ways, Inspector. A few like-minded souls find the clamour of modern life too much for our delicate constitutions. My brother and the good doctor have learned to indulge me. I hope you will, too."

In truth, I had only seen Mycroft a handful of times in the years I had known Holmes and our relationship was affable without being what one would call close. I suppose, if I'm honest in the matter, my nose had been somewhat put out of joint when he had been the one Holmes had entrusted with the secret of his survival after the Reichenbach incident, leaving me to grieve all those months over what I assumed was his death. Having said that, I perfectly understood and had long since accepted my friend's motives.

To say that Mycroft Holmes was a large man was a considerable understatement. He was built on a gargantuan scale. Holmes was tall—an inch or two over six feet—and his lean frame made him seem even taller but his elder brother, though perhaps only an inch or so more in height, gave the impression of being absolutely massive. The face was large and, although it was not obvious at first glance, closer inspection revealed certain similarities. There was the same sharpness of expression on the rare occasions that his attention was engaged and the eyes—a peculiarly light, watery grey—had in their depths that distant, introspective look I had encountered in only one other man and that was Sherlock Holmes when he was exerting his full powers.

This was the formidable man who was now ushering us, like some maiden aunt, into a rather shabby little room that completely deserved the title lettered over the door—STRANGERS' ROOM.

As he closed the door behind us, Mycroft spoke in a normal tone for the first time since we had entered the cloister he called a club. Looking ostentatiously at his watch again, he said briskly—"I can give you just seventeen minutes. For you to burst in at this time of day, I can only assume there is some matter which you believe to be of some small import?"

And a corner of one eyebrow was raised interrogatively some quarter of an inch from the perpendicular.

All of which was wasted on Holmes, who had played this game before. Taking the photograph from his pocket, he thrust it into his brother's hand.

"My dear Mycroft, I was merely wondering what you could tell us about this . . ."

Mycroft adjusted a pair of *pince-nez* and held the photo up to the light.

At which point the universe imploded. Or rather, to be exact, Mycroft's eyebrow shot up a further quarter inch. Then, very carefully, he laid it down on the room's central table.

"Wait here," he said in a tone so different from his normal one that I felt a chill tiptoe up my spine. And then the door closed softly behind him.

For the next few minutes none of us exchanged a word. There seemed to be nothing to say. The only one to move was Holmes, who looked once more at the photograph without picking it up and then began to drum his fingers on it. I found myself concentrating on the rhythm to see if it had any specific meaning but, as far as I could tell, it did not.

"I believe the expression is—'Snap!' "

Somehow Mycroft had re-entered the room without our hearing and I was reminded how light on his feet he could be for such a large man.

Now he laid something down side by side with the photograph.

It was an identical copy—except that this time the image of Sir Simon Briggs was untouched.

This time another figure had been literally "de-faced." This one wore a sweater with the capital letter "P."

As three heads bent as one over the twin images, I heard Mycroft say—"Briggs, too?"

Holmes straightened up.

"And 'P'?"

"I'm afraid so. Victor Ian Pelham—known to his friends as V.I.P., which always pleased him greatly, since he had ambitions in that direction. To be accurate, I should say Victor Pelham, M.P. A rising figure in the Liberal Party. Many of his colleagues felt he might well fill Gladstone's shoes one of these days but that, alas, we shall now never know."

He answered his brother's questioning glance.

"Victor Pelham died this afternoon on the floor of the House of Commons. He appears to have been poisoned."

As Mycroft began speaking, we had all found ourselves chairs around the table and now we sat there like guests at a séance.

It was Lestrade who reacted first.

"So that must have been all that kerfuffle that was going on as I was leaving for Baker Street. I heard something about the House of Commons but I thought it must be one of those demonstrations they're always having there these days."

"But before I get into that—what about *this?*"

And Mycroft picked up the "A" photograph between his finger and thumb, as though he thought it might well be contaminated.

For the next few minutes Holmes and I described what had happened up in Scotland. By the time we had finished—with the occasional "Lumme" or "Strike me!" interruption from Lestrade and total inscrutable silence on the part of Mycroft—the room was beginning to grow dark.

Mycroft did not even bother to consult his watch but simply rang for a steward and ordered a welcome round of whisky and soda. When it had been brought and we were once again alone, he appeared to have come to a conclusion.

"Well, gentlemen, since we appear to have arrived at the same point in the maze, albeit by differing routes, it would seem sensible to compare notes.

"I was apprised of this late this afternoon"— and he picked up the Pelham photo—"in my governmental capacity . . ."

Exactly what that "capacity" was I was never to learn. Suffice it to say that there was little that went on in Her Majesty's Government in which Mycroft Holmes was not involved to one degree or another. Whatever strings were pulled, they seemed to end up in his hands. I remember Holmes once telling me with distinct admiration in his voice that "occasionally he *is* the British

Government . . . again and again his word has decided the national policy."

It was perfectly credible, therefore, that faced with such an *outré* occurrence, the powers-that-be should have placed the matter in this safest of safe pair of hands.

"Victor was due to present the Opposition view on penal reform at approximately four p.m.," Mycroft continued. "He was, like many of us . . ."—and here he glanced pointedly at Holmes—"a creature of meticulous habit. When delivering a prepared address such as this, he would invariably bring into the House and set beside him his notes, a carafe of water and a glass. Apparently, when called upon to speak this afternoon, he took up his place, arranged his notes in his usual fashion, poured himself a glass of water, took a sip, then began to speak.

"Half way through his first sentence, he gasped, clutched his throat and fell forward. As you may imagine—pandemonium ensued. He was taken to the infirmary but was pronounced dead on arrival. Scotland Yard is naturally conducting an autopsy but preliminary examination suggests one of the faster acting poisons, such as cyanide, perhaps masked by the touch of lemon Victor liked to add to the water.

"I was sent for post haste and was the only one allowed into his private room . . ."

"And what did you find?" Holmes was leaning

forward intently, his bony fingers clasped in front of him.

"The room had clearly been searched but not particularly disturbed. The only things that had obviously been rearranged were . . ."

"His books," Holmes finished for him.

"Just so." It was as much a question as a comment but Holmes motioned to his brother to continue.

"Victor liked to keep everything in logical order. He was something of a fanatic in that regard. It is inconceivable that he would have allowed his personal copies of *Hansard* to be placed on the shelf out of their chronological order."

"But his personal quarters told a different story?"

If Mycroft's amused glance had needed words, they would undoubtedly have been of the order of—"So my little brother has not lost his edge?" But there were none and he continued . . .

"Victor keeps—kept—a suite of rooms just off Smith Square for when the House was in session. I made my way straight there and—as you rightly suspected, Sherlock—found them in chaos. Whoever was searching for—whatever they were searching for—had been at no pains in this case to cover their tracks. Victor's possessions were strewn around everywhere and . . ."—another glance at Holmes—"particular attention had been paid to the books."

"And the 'P'?"

"Crudely traced in ink on the top of his desk. Quite ruined the leather, I'm afraid.

"And lying in the middle of the floor was—this photograph." Here he picked it up and looked at it thoughtfully.

"With which you were already thoroughly familiar," Holmes added matter of factly.

Mycroft paused for a long moment, then spoke over our heads into the far distance.

"The men in that photograph were all students at Christ Church College, Oxford in what our American friends would call the Class of 1867. As you will doubtless remember, Sherlock, there is something in the air during those three student years that brings out a certain childish quality in what are presumed to be grown men . . ."

Looking at my friend, I doubted very much that he had experienced any such thing at first hand—and I suspected Mycroft knew that perfectly well, too, from his ironic tone.

"The young men in this photograph considered themselves a kind of elite, superior to their fellows in every conceivable way, especially in brain power. The rules of ordinary society were not meant for them, even though, in reality, they were perfectly conventional in their everyday behaviour.

"As a gesture of their individuality they determined to form an exclusive club that by its very name would proclaim separation from the common horde.

"There were seven of them—so they would call themselves The Seven Sinners. Each of them would take on the name of whichever of the Seven Deadly Sins he thought most appropriate to his nature. Each of the initial letters you see on their sweaters stands for their chosen name.

"Poor Victor was always a little full of himself, convinced he was going places. Fortunately, he was aware of it and could take a certain amount of ragging. He was 'P' for Pride . . ."

"And Briggs, being the would-be financial entrepreneur, no doubt saw himself as Avarice— hence the 'A'?" Holmes interrupted.

"Correct."

"And the others?" I prompted.

Mycroft examined the photograph again, although I sensed he needed no reminding of its details.

"The chubby little fellow is Pierre Pascal. French, obviously, and the son of a famous chef. I believe he returned to Paris and went into the family business. Pierre insisted on claiming 'G' for Gluttony. Said it was a matter of professional honour."

He smiled slightly at the recollection.

"Now, Bob McKay here was a dark horse . . ." He indicated an earnest, thin featured young man wearing the letter "L." "You'd have thought butter wouldn't have melted in his mouth at the time but in later years I hear he got himself involved in one or two—shall we say 'compromising' situations involving ladies, several of whom were married, and dropped out of sight. We thought Bob's opting for 'L' for Lust was a great joke at the time but . . ."

"Perhaps it was the title that put the idea into his head?" said Holmes and there was a brief twinkle in those deep set eyes. Then, as if to make amends for his levity—"And who is the heavy set young man glowering at the camera?"

"Ah, now, *he* was aptly named. George Edward Challenger . . ."

"Not *the* Professor Challenger?" I could not help exclaiming.

"You mean there are *two!*" Now it was Mycroft's turn to introduce a lighter note. "But you're quite right, Doctor. The very same Professor Challenger, zoologist, anthropologist and explorer, like his father before him—the bane of every scientific society for his criticism of what he considers their pusillanimous methods and the darling of the gutter Press for the head-lines he creates . . ."

"When he isn't throwing them bodily down his stairs and having to be arrested."

We all turned in Lestrade's direction. It was the first thing he had said since we had entered the

56

room but this was clearly something about which he had had first hand experience.

"The man has the strength of a raging bull and the temper to go with it," he continued. "I've known it take four of my men to hold him."

"In short, Doctor, yes, *the* Professor Challenger—even then a self-styled Renaissance Man. It won't surprise you to hear that he chose 'R' for Rage."

"And the smaller man standing next to him and looking at Challenger rather than the camera?" asked Holmes.

"Challenger's *doppelgänger*," Mycroft replied. "John Summerlee. Now, of course, also *Professor* Summerlee. Right through university and ever since he has dogged Challenger's footsteps . . ."

"If I am not mistaken, it could be said that he has *challenged* Challenger at every turn," Holmes interrupted.

"Both professionally and personally. If Challenger says 'black,' Summerlee insists it's 'white.' They even argue about the time of day. It is, I confess, the strangest of relationships and yet the strangest thing of all is that, deep down, they are the closest of friends. They need each other. The one *defines* the other."

"Rather like Watson and myself?" said Holmes and I fancy he was only half joking, which pleased me more than a little.

Mycroft let the remark pass.

"He was not best pleased to be assigned 'E' for Envy, but since it was the only designation left, he had little choice. Naturally, he blamed Challenger for that, too."

It was then that I noticed something that should have been obvious to me earlier.

"The seventh man. He has no initial letter."

"Indeed, he has not, Doctor. Evan Staunton was—how can I put it?—*with* the group but not *of* the group. Upon its foundation it had been determined that it could have but seven members at any one time. Doubtless there could be any number of additional deadly sins that fertile young minds could devise but the group was happy enough with the conceit of the original seven.

"Consequently, young Staunton remained a supplicant, permitted to join in certain of the group functions but denied full membership privileges—for whatever *they* were worth."

"So he never became one of the seven?" Lestrade sounded puzzled. "Then what's he doing in the photograph?"

Mycroft looked thoughtful. "No, he never did. When McKay was sent down—after an unfortunate business involving the wife of one of the dons . . ."

"A self-fulfilling prophecy, by the sounds of it," I offered.

". . . at that point Staunton renewed his

application. Rather embarrassingly, it was black-balled. Unanimously. Staunton took it very hard and dropped out of the college's social life completely. Some time later we heard that he had gone down.

"Personally, I thought the whole business was rather juvenile. After all, what did we have but a dining club with a silly name. I'm sure we'd all be rather ashamed to admit to it today."

"Except that there are two less of you to have that option open to them," said Holmes sharply. "And when you use the word 'we,' you are merely confirming what had been implicit for much of your narrative. You, I take it, were . . ."

" 'S' for Sloth." And had the light in the Strangers' Room been brighter, I would have sworn that Mycroft blushed.

CHAPTER FOUR

By rights *I* should have been the seventh man in that picture. It transpired, however, that Staunton, who was supposed to have been taking the portrait, didn't quite know how to work the camera and so it was left to me. Quite a good effort, even if I do say so myself."

Holmes had risen from his chair and was pacing the room, his hands clasped behind his back—a sure sign that a line of thought was preoccupying him.

"And you say that Staunton dropped out of the university. Have you any idea what happened to him?"

"Not really. I did hear that he tried his hand as a war correspondent. Alas, there always seem to be an ample supply of them in this Empire on which the sun supposedly never sets. There was talk of his being seen in Afghanistan and India—your old haunts, Doctor—but that was years ago."

"And what happened to The Seven Sinners?" I interjected. "Did you all meet again over the years? Annual reunions . . . passwords, secret handshakes—that sort of thing?"

"I'm sorry to disappoint you, Doctor, but I'm afraid nothing of the kind. You are confusing the Sinners with the Masons. As I say, it was a misconceived idea in the first place and it soon palled. All of the members were highly intelligent and soon regretted their rather pretentious behaviour. But since we were all vain, too, we found it difficult to come out and say so. The consequence was that we began to pick foolish quarrels with one another. What with one thing and another, the club simply fell apart and we all went our separate ways. Nothing was actually said but there was certainly no reason for any of us to keep up contact with any of the rest. I have had a limited amount of contact with Victor Pelham, admittedly, but strictly on Commons business. As for the rest . . ."

It was Lestrade who spoke next. Mopping his brow with a none-too-clean bandana—adequate ventilation not being high on the Diogenes' list of amenities—he turned towards the man who had solved so many of his conundrums for him.

"It's a rum do and no mistake. What do *you* make of it, Mr. 'Olmes?"

Holmes stopped his pacing and spoke from the gathering gloom.

"If the club were to be reconvened—which I sincerely hope will not be the case—it would have to add an eighth sin. 'M' for Murder.

"Two of its members have been murdered, ostensibly for what they were thought to have possessed but, in fact, apparently did not. From this I believe it is fair to deduce that it is a singular object and that the murderer will continue until he finds it. However, the *means* of the killings and particularly the use of the initial letters suggest something else. Our killer wishes to send a personal message to the rest of The Seven Sinners . . ."

"And that message is . . . ?" I asked.

"Whichever of you has it, I shall find it." He paused and looked at Mycroft. "And yet it may very well be that none of you knows what 'it' is or that you have it.

"Tell me, Mycroft—what do we know of the whereabouts of the other four Sinners?"

"Pascal, I presume, is in his native Paris and that is something we can easily check. McKay, as I say, is something of a recluse and may take a little more finding, but I have little doubt that our resources . . ." He left the sentence unfinished. If McKay was breathing Her Majesty's good fresh air, Mycroft's "resources" would run him to ground.

"Challenger and Summerlee, I believe, are off on one of their endless expeditions up the Zambesi or Limpopo or somewhere such. Again, I shall make enquiries as to their itinerary."

"Which leaves your good and very visible self," Holmes added. Then seeing his brother's expression. "No, Mycroft, I would strongly advise against your taking this lightly. You may be above the petty concerns of running the country but I doubt that will cut too much ice with a man as daring and determined as the one we are now seeking.

"How, for instance, did he gain access to Pelham's room in the House? The Palace of Westminster is not exactly a public thoroughfare, unless you have changed the rules recently?"

Mycroft looked thoughtful.

"Now that you mention it, Victor's Private Secretary did mention that he had a visitor not long before he was due to make his speech. The Secretary suggested that, as the gentleman did not have an appointment and in view of the importance of the occasion, it might be preferable to ask him to return on a subsequent occasion."

"And why did this not happen?"

"Apparently, the visitor asked him to pass on the message—'Ask him if he can not spare a minute for a poor sinner who has repented?' When he heard the message—the Secretary said—Victor looked puzzled for a moment, then said the man was to be shown in. 'Tell him that, of course, I can spare a minute—two, if necessary.'"

"Did he recall anything else? Think, Mycroft—the slightest detail may be important."

"Ah, now I recall. When the man entered the room, he heard Victor say—'Oh, it's *you?*' And then the door shut behind them. Later he thought he heard raised voices when he knocked to advise Victor that he was due in the Chamber. Since it was his duty to accompany his master and hand him his notes for the speech, he did not see the man actually leave the building."

"Leaving our 'Sinner' ample time and opportunity to search Pelham's rooms and leave his signature. I think you will find, Mycroft, that he went straight from there to the Smith Square accommodation and ransacked that."

Mycroft's expression told me that, once again, Holmes had surmised correctly.

"But 'ow did he manage to poison this M.P. feller?"

Holmes made a dismissive gesture.

"A mere detail, Lestrade. I would assume Pelham used the standard water carafe made available to all members—in which case it would be simplicity itself to make a simple substitution of a 'doctored' carafe while he was temporarily distracted. Had he used a carafe that had an out of the ordinary design, it would be easy enough for someone in the Visitors' Gallery to discern that fact—and I'm sure our friend has been a frequent 'Visitor' in recent days or weeks. Then the poison would have to have been introduced during the course of the 'visit.' In either event, arranging the death posed no significant problem for him.

"The question with which we must now concern ourselves is—who is the next victim to be? 'M'—as I now prefer to call him—has killed twice and on both occasions in what can only be termed a dramatic fashion. More than that, each of the murders is orchestrated to the 'sin' appropriate to the individual concerned. The financier is immured with his booty; the high-flying politician is the victim of his own *hubris*. It may be that the murders are incidental to his search. Once he has ascertained that the subject does not have what he wants, that man knows his purpose and cannot be allowed to live to tell it and almost certainly warn others.

"And yet I wonder . . ." His voice trailed away, as if he were lost in his own speculation. Then he snapped abruptly back to life.

"Well, gentlemen, we shall not find our man by sitting in the comfort of these luxurious surroundings. Lestrade, I have a small favour to ask."

"Right you are, Mr. 'Olmes."

"Could I ask you to use your good offices to have a section of this photograph copied . . ."— and here he picked up Mycroft's copy and indicated an area with his forefinger—". . . and enlarged as much as possible without losing the clarity of the image? Time, I need hardly add, is of the essence.

"Mycroft, I mean it most sincerely when I urge you to take every precaution concerning your personal safety. I would advise you to stay here at the club for the time being and not to go about your daily business unaccompanied. Your acquaintance is wide and among it, almost certainly known to you—though not necessarily by his overt identity—is our killer.

"Come, Watson, Baker Street calls. And since my parsimonious brother is clearly not minded to offer us dinner, we must hope that Mrs. Hudson's good plain cooking will suffice."

And he swept from the room, leaving the rest of us to follow in his wake.

CHAPTER FIVE

If Mrs. Hudson was put out by our returning unexpectedly with a request from Holmes for "Your finest cold table, Mrs. Hudson, and a bottle of the '92 Fleurie Dr. Watson was keeping for a special occasion!"—she showed no outward sign of it. Within ten minutes of our arrival she was bustling around our sitting room, pointedly pushing Holmes's assorted paraphernalia out of the way so that the dining table could be put to its intended use.

"One of these days, Mr. Holmes, I do declare you'll be drinking one of those chemical things of yours instead of your wine. And then where'll you be?"

"I shall probably be complaining to St. Peter about the quality of the vintage, Mrs. Hudson. But you may be sure I shall not seek to lay the blame at your door. Even if we don't show it, Doctor Watson and I are eternally grateful for your tolerance of our funny little ways, aren't we, Watson?"

This seemed to mollify the good lady and she was smiling as she left with her tray. I thought I heard her murmur something about—"There's only *one* person around here has funny ways that *I* know of . . ." which brought a smile to my face, too, for I chose to assume she did not mean *me*.

Hardly had the door closed behind her when it opened again.

"You made me forget this letter that came for you while you were out, Mr. Holmes." And she laid an envelope on the table next to Holmes's plate before leaving again.

Holmes manoeuvred it around with his knife, turning it over so that he could see both sides without picking it up—his invariable habit with missives about which he entertained the slightest doubt.

His post bag, as might be imagined, is an unorthodox one, to say the least. His correspondents range from the highest in the land—indeed, the world—to schoolgirls in Penzance or post masters in Walsall, all convinced that he and only he has the answer to their concerns. Each of them in due time he feels duty bound to answer and the schoolgirl is quite likely to be answered before the sir.

However—and I date this to the Moriarty years—he has lately taken to this more careful initial approach. On one occasion a package contained a primitive explosive device, which he detected by its odour. On another there was a scorpion, fortunately deceased by the time it made its entrance.

Now, having decided the letter contained neither of these undesirable offerings, he picked it up by opposite corners. He then proceeded to hold it up to the light from the window, shake it and finally sniff it, before putting it down in front of me.

"Now, Watson. You have seen the envelope, as have I. What do you deduce from it?"

It was a game Holmes liked to play every now and then—usually to divert his mind from whatever was preoccupying him at the moment—and I invariably indulged him. I copied his actions precisely, though, to be honest, I was not at all sure what they told me.

"Heavy paper. Obviously expensive. Therefore, your correspondent is someone of means. Probably a woman. No man would use stationery of a pastel hue. Not an aristocrat, either. I have yet to see someone who had the right to use a title who failed to emblazon their crest on every available surface . . ."

I examined the handwriting more closely.

"The delicacy of the script also suggests a woman's hand and something in the shaping of the letters makes me feel she is not from these islands. I would suggest a Continental hand. Other than that, I can deduce nothing."

And I sat back, perfectly well pleased with myself. Sometimes I feel that Holmes makes too much of these little parlour tricks of his.

"Capital, old fellow. This time you have really scratched the surface . . ."

I was basking in his all-too-rare praise when he continued—

"Unfortunately, you have missed those clues that tell us the more specific facts."

"Such as?"

"The configuration of the letters certainly has a European influence. The lady in question has spent time there, without a doubt. Yet the European penmanship is overlaid on something more fundamental. The rounding of certain letters—in fact, the calligraphy as a whole—leaves a distinct impression of certain forms of Indian script.

"As you know, I have made a small study of handwriting and in my judgement this lady was born and raised in the Indian sub-continent, before travelling to—Paris, as a guess, possibly Switzerland—to 'finish' her education.

"That deduction is aided by the fact that, in addressing the envelope, she rested her wrist on the corner of it and thus left the impress of the bracelet she was wearing. If you hold it up to the light, you will see the faint pattern of the metal, which appears to be a stylised design of braided ropes—no, I'm wrong—of interwoven serpents . . ."

"A traditional Hindu motif," I interjected.

"Indeed."

"So an Indian lady of means who has lived in Europe is writing to you?"

"Not *an* Indian lady, my dear fellow. That is the most obvious thing you missed. *The* Indian lady. She clearly has a marked preference for the colour green. As you see, even the pastel shade of her envelope is green and if you will take the trouble to smell it . . ."

I did as he suggested. And, indeed, there was a distinct hint of that remarkable perfume I had come to associate with the Emerald Lady.

"Well, Holmes, now that you have dissected her, aren't you going to see what she has to *say?*" I asked, I'm afraid rather huffily.

There was the vestige of a smile on Holmes's face as he extracted a single folded sheet of paper and smoothed it flat. He examined it briefly before passing it to me.

In that same rounded hand I read . . .

"THAT WHICH IS LOST MUST BE
  FOUND.
THAT WHICH IS OURS MUST BE
  RETURNED."

Not surprisingly, the letter was unsigned but at the bottom—again in green—was a seal. It bore the image of two serpents' heads facing in opposite directions. There was malevolence in the drawing and I found myself shivering slightly as I looked at it.

Holmes's voice brought me back to the real world.

"Strange, is it not, the way we react so differently to the Maker's many creatures. If those had been two lambs, two horses or even two lions, you would have experienced very different emotions. But two *snakes* . . . Perhaps the Garden of Eden has something to do with the dread and the ambiguity.

"Be a good fellow and make a long arm in the direction of my reference books. The second volume under 'S,' I fancy . . ."

I did as he asked and for the next several minutes he was engrossed in the contents, occasionally reading something aloud—as much for his own edification as for mine.

"SMALL, Jonathan . . . You hardly need reminding of *him,* old fellow . . . ?"

And, indeed, I did not. One of the Four in the adventure I had related under the title of *The Sign of Four*, Small—admittedly under duress—had conspired to steal the Agra Treasure. After years of penal servitude, he had returned to England in pursuit of what he now considered rightfully his. His eventual capture, after a hair-raising boat pursuit along the Thames, had almost shortened my life and Holmes's. Still, I had that adventure to thank for my introduction to Mary Morstan— my darling Mary who was to be my wife for such a tragically short time . . .

"THE SMITH-MORTIMER SUCCESSION CASE . . . Not without its points of interest . . ." Holmes was referring to a complex case from the previous year. "One of these days, my dear chap, we must unleash your literary powers on that one. But not quite yet, I fancy, not quite yet . . .

"Ah, here we are . . . SNAKES AND SERPENTS . . .

"Hm, most interesting. They appear to have evolved some one hundred and thirty million years ago—which puts *homo sapiens* firmly in his place . . . Let's see—two and a half thousand different species of which three hundred are venomous and more than fifty dangerous to humans . . . one of which can spit its venom into the eye of its prey ten feet way, paralysing the nervous system. Be careful where you tread, Watson!

"Ah, now we come to it . . . The Serpent as Religious Symbol . . . There seems to be scarcely a religion worth the name that *doesn't* find a place of honour for our slippery friend. A highly complex symbol, indeed.

"It represents ambivalence—both male and female, light and dark, life and death. Violent destruction on the one hand and yet the periodical shedding of the skin also represents renewal and resurrection. But I see that the dark side tends to dominate overall.

"Let me quote—'It is knowledge, power,

guile, cunning and corruption. It is Fate itself, swift as disaster, deliberate as retribution, incomprehensible as destiny.' In short old fellow, not an adversary to be taken lightly.

"Now, what have we here? *Two* serpents . . . 'Two serpents together symbolize the opposites of dualism which are ultimately united. Wound round each other they are Time and Fate, the two great binding powers.'

"May I see that envelope again, please, Watson?"

I passed it to him and he compared it closely to something in what he was reading.

"As I thought, the snake depicted here is the King Cobra, the *uraeus*, the deadliest snake known to man and the supreme symbol in Eastern religions of divine knowledge, wisdom and eternal power. A pair of them entwined are the guardians of the threshold, the keepers of all material and spiritual treasures and the Waters of Life . . . protectors and servants of the all-powerful Earth Goddess."

"The Earth Goddess"—I had a sudden vision of the Emerald Lady and she looked troubled.

Holmes marked his place with a slip of paper and replaced the volume on the shelf.

"Something tells me we shall have need to consult this again," he said soberly. "The fact that it sounds like so much mumbo-jumbo to our good Church of England ears does not detract from the fact that others think very differently and pursue their beliefs, no matter what the cost."

He sat back in his chair and steepled his fingers in that familiar fashion that seemed to aid contemplation for him.

"Now just what did seven schoolboyish English sinners do to provoke forces such as these—that is the question we must address, Watson.

"We have much to ponder on, old fellow. A poisoned M.P., a suffocated financier and a sloth disturbed from his hibernation—not to mention an Emerald Lady and her entourage. Where is the common link? These are such stuff as dreams are made on and most certainly a three pipe problem.

"I bid you good night, Watson."

And with that he gathered together all the cushions he could find and arranged them on the floor. This was my indication that he wished to be alone to ponder the case and I took it gratefully. The Glorious Twelfth had been all very well but the days since had left it a mere memory of something that had happened in the distant past.

I made for my bed and was asleep as soon as my head touched the pillow.

Holmes's parting remark may have had something to do with it. I suppose, because dreams most certainly did come.

I was walking along a jungle path and treading very gingerly indeed—presumably because of

Holmes's warning—when out of the bushes, towering over me and waving its hooded head menacingly, was an enormous King Cobra. As I recoiled, there was a hiss behind me and I turned to see an identical serpent. But the strangest thing was that each of them had a man's face. The first I recognised as that of Briggs and somehow I knew that the second must be Pelham.

The hissing rose in volume and just when I was sure they were both ready to strike, a woman's voice said—"No, *he* is not the one." Then, right in front of me, materialised the image of the Emerald Lady, except that she appeared to be floating well above the ground. Now she seemed to be beckoning to me but, as I moved towards her, the image receded until it faded away entirely.

Now I was in a clearing. In the middle of it was a small multi-coloured hill, made up of what I now saw were cushions of different shapes and sizes. On the top of the hill, sitting cross legged and looking for all the world like the Tenniel illustration of the Caterpillar in *Alice*, complete with hookah, was Holmes.

As I approached the hill and looked up at him, he leaned over and frowned at me.

"We can't have you dreaming the day away, Watson. Not when we have a clue to pursue . . .

". . . a clue to pursue . . . a clue to pursue . . ."

It sounded like a children's nursery rhyme. Why couldn't I remember the rest of it? And now my whole body was beginning to shake. Surely not another touch of the old malaria?

And then I was sitting up in bed with Holmes standing over me, smiling like the Cheshire Cat with the cream and I realised it was he who had been shaking me awake.

"Come along, old fellow. I need your help. Leave the embraces of dusky maidens for now..." Could the man now read my dreams? "Lestrade has something to show us."

The bedroom door closed behind him.

When, a few minutes later, I entered the sitting room it was to find Holmes and Lestrade leaning over something spread on the table among the debris of breakfast. Even if Holmes had sat up half the night with his "three pipe problem," it had clearly not affected his appetite. I could see the remains of kidneys and bacon and was about to summon Mrs. Hudson, to see if she could provide more of the same, when Holmes reached out and pulled me over to join them.

"Tell me, old fellow, what do you make of this?" And he gestured towards what I now saw to be a large photograph. A moment's examination showed it to be an enlargement of the picture of The Seven Sinners we had been studying the previous day. This time the picture had been cropped, so that only the central portion remained.

Three of the young men could be seen clearly and they were the ones seated in the centre of the group.

On the left was Victor Pelham, thin faced and smugly aristocratic. His expression said that he was naturally above all such nonsense but was prepared to indulge the others in it for the time being.

On the extreme right was a chubby young man who already bore all the signs of being an extremely chubby older man. The face was essentially bland but there was a twinkle in the eyes that spoke of humour and good comradeship.

"Pierre Pascal," Holmes volunteered, " '*le jeune gastronome.*' "

But it was the figure in the centre that held my eye. I had only seen that face before when a frenzied knife cut had almost obliterated it in a photograph and when it stared up at me in death from the floor of his inner sanctum.

The young Simon Briggs looked out at the world as if he owned it—and it seemed to be his clear ambition that he would acquire as much of it as he could. If avarice was ever written on a face in embryo, it was written there.

Holmes once again anticipated my own thoughts.

"If I were a superstitious man, gentlemen, I would be inclined to believe that either these men were uniquely qualified by nature to form their society and assume their particular roles—or that the fact of belonging to it impressed their roles upon their very souls. But then, fortunately, I am not a superstitious man."

Then I noticed that there was something different about Briggs. He was holding something in his lap. It had been too small in the original photo but now I could see that it was a book of some sort.

"Try this, Doctor." And Lestrade held out a magnifying glass.

Now I could see that the book was bound in some fine leather and on the front cover there was a complex design. At first I thought it must be purely decorative but on a closer examination . . .

"Good heavens, Holmes—the twin cobras!"

"Precisely, Watson. And . . . ?"

I gave the glass a rub and looked again. What I had assumed to be a series of elaborate curlicues and swirls now took on more specific meaning.

"Sanskrit," I said decisively. I've never been one to bother much about dead languages, except for the Latin I'd needed for my medical training, but I'd seen plenty of this one during my time in India.

"That's just what Mr. 'Olmes said before you came in, Doctor. But what's this sand script when it's at 'ome?"

Holmes picked up the photograph and ran his long fingers lightly over the inscription.

"The name given to the language written and spoken in the northern part of the sub-continent around 1,000 B.C. Many of the sacred Hindu texts are written in it. It died out over the centuries during the ebb and flow of successive invading cultures but recently scholars have reconstructed it, so that it may be studied once more.

"I think we may safely assume that this book— whatever it is—is what the Emerald Lady—as Watson so gallantly calls her—and her retinue are looking for. We must now find out *why*."

"But what's all this got to do with them— those—Sinner fellers?"

"She clearly believes—from the evidence of this photograph—that one of them has it in his possession and is determined to retrieve it any cost. The fact that Briggs is holding it in the picture presumably gave her reason to assume that he would be a likely place to look first. Since that obviously proved not to be the case, the others must be presumed to be equally at risk and in random order. Pelham proved to be the most visible—with the result we have seen. And yet . . ."

"And yet *what,* Holmes?"

"There is more to it, Watson. Just as the twin serpents are inseparably entwined, there is another thread to this plot."

"Shouldn't we be out looking for this Emerald Lady?" Lestrade asked.

"I think not, Lestrade—at least, not for the present," Holmes replied thoughtfully. "Our priority must be to keep a close watch on the surviving Sinners. Until and unless our Indian friends find what they are looking for, we need hardly look for *them*. We have only to bait our hook and they will come to *us*.

"Briggs and Pelham have, so to speak, paid the price of their respective 'sins'; Challenger, Summerlee, Pascal—and presumably, Staunton— are safely out of the country . . . which leaves only my brother and the mysterious Mr. McKay to worry about. Incidentally, Lestrade, have your men had any luck in tracking McKay down yet?"

"Not yet, Mr. 'Olmes. You'd be surprised 'ow many McKays, McKees and McCoys there are in the greater London area but, if he's here, we'll find him soon enough, don't you worry."

"I'm sure you will, Lestrade. Watson will tell you that I have never doubted your tenacity of purpose, have I, Watson?"

I murmured my assent. It didn't seem necessary to add that there had been occasions when it had been the only commendation of the Inspector's performance my friend felt able to summon up.

"And now, if you will excuse us, Dr. Watson and I have a visit we must pay."

"Oh, and where's that, Holmes?"

"To the British Museum, old fellow. It's time we brushed up our Sanskrit . . ."

CHAPTER SIX

The British Museum has perched on its Bloomsbury site like a comfortable beehive since 1753 with the worker bees of all nations happily buzzing in and out about their business. By late morning Holmes and I were two of them.

I freely admit I find the place a little daunting on the rare occasions I've visited it. All that antiquity is too much for a simple soldier to take in. Give me something I can get my hands on any time. Holmes, however, revels in it and, when a case demands research, I have known him spend days at a time there, returning to Baker Street overflowing with enthusiasm for some abstruse subject that he then tries to explain to me. This is a process that invariably ends with him raising his eyebrows in despair with the cry—"Watson, I declare you have no soul!"

This morning, as we climbed the steps to the main door, he clearly knew his destination. Instead of proceeding straight ahead to the main Reading Room, he set a determined pace through a maze of departments.

It was as though we were on a Cook's tour of the past. One moment we were in the heart of Ancient Egypt, as we passed among mummies, sarcophagi and temple friezes. The next we were in the glory that was Greece and a moment later, or so it seemed, Greece had been conquered by the might of Rome. If I had taken more notice during my history lessons at school, I'm sure it would have all fitted into place. As it was, I was left feeling more than a little diminished. In their day each of these civilisations had ruled the known world and the men whose artifacts were now gathering dust thousands of miles away from their homeland had assumed that their various gods had intended that it would always be that way. Would the mighty *British* Empire inevitably come to the same resolution? Surely not.

As I was contemplating such weighty matters, Holmes came to a sudden stop.

"Here we are, my dear fellow. The font of knowledge."

We were in one of the side passages and one that was rather dimly lit. Presumably this by way of being an economy measure, since I had the distinct impression that we were in one of the Museum's by-ways rather than its highways.

We stood in front of a door with the legend in faded gilt letters—ORIENTAL & ASIATIC MSS.

Holmes rapped firmly on the door. Silence.

I scrutinised the smaller type—HOURS 10.00 A.M.—5.00 P.M.

"There should be someone there at this hour, Holmes. Try again."

He did so and now we heard a shuffling sound from within and a moment later a quavering voice called for us to come in.

Like everything else about the Museum, the room was bigger than one had expected. Tall shelves piled high with boxes and folders receded into the far distance and bore a distinct air of the accumulated dust of generations. Tables were submerged with further piles of paper, presumably awaiting the ministrations of a cataloguer.

Then from behind a row of shelves a man appeared, adjusting a pair of wire-rimmed *pince-nez* and for the second time that day I was put in mind of *Alice*, as he had in his hand a pocket watch, which he shook and put next to one ear. If he had said—"Oh, my fur and whiskers!" I should have known him for the White Rabbit.

"A thousand pardons, gentlemen, but I was deep in an early Middle Eastern text and did not hear your knock. I do hope I haven't kept you waiting too long but in my field—as I'm sure you can imagine—time is almost entirely past tense." And he gave a little laugh to emphasise his witticism.

"Pray don't apologise, my dear Mr.—" Holmes raised a hand in polite protest.

"Hinckley."

"Mr. Hinckley. My colleague, Doctor Watson and I are grateful to you for seeing us without the benefit of an appointment but our business is of an urgent nature."

Then with a most untypical, almost roguish display of bonhomie, Holmes leaned over to peer at the manuscript Hinckley had tucked under his arm.

"I wonder if I might . . . ?"

And with that he had plucked the document away and was peering at it intently, for all the world like a desiccated professor himself.

"Ah, as I thought—Early Armenian. Fifth Century B.C., I'll be bound. No, I'm wrong—late fourth century. Oh, my dear fellow, if only the world knew the linguistic sophistication of these people. I envy you your lot in life, I really do, locked away with minds of this calibre. Perhaps on some future occasion, you might find the time to compare notes. I have some early Coptic scrolls on which I would value your expert opinion."

He carefully replaced the document under the man's arm. Hinckley, I must say, looked a trifle surprised at my friend's behaviour, as well he might.

"Now," Holmes rushed on with the breathless enthusiasm of the true academic, "I'm sure this won't take two seconds of your time. My colleague and I are anxious—for reasons I won't bore you with—to identify the book in this photograph . . ."

He took out of an envelope the enlargement we had been studying and handed it reverently to Hinckley, as if it were the Old Testament itself.

There was a glint as the librarian adjusted his glasses. It was the lens catching the light but I could have sworn that there was something in his eye that had not been there before, as he examined it.

"There it is, do you see?" said Holmes, poking the relevant section with a bony finger, though the book was quite evident. "We're virtually certain that the script is Sanskrit but we need to know what it says."

Hinckley pursed his lips and made that little humming noise that seems inseparable from all professional pronouncements. Having peered at the photo for several moments, he handed it back to my friend with a shake of the head.

"I'm sorry to disappoint you, gentlemen, but what you have here—or rather, what that gentleman in the picture has there—is simply a manual of botany. A common household item at the time."

"Which would be?"

"Oh—um—third century B.C."

"Well, Watson, I'm afraid you win your bet." He turned to Hinckley with a conspiratorial wink—quite unlike Holmes. "The Doctor and I have had a small bet, you see. I was convinced the book must have some religious significance but he insisted it did not. I'm afraid you have cost me the price of a good lunch. Doctor Watson is not to be fobbed off with less. Anyway, thank you for your time, Mr. Hinckley. And now we really must let Mr. Hinckley get back to fifth century Armenia. Come, Watson . . ."

And before I knew it, we were out of the door and back in the corridor with Holmes hurrying me along with his hand under my elbow, until we had turned the corner.

"What on earth was all that about, Holmes?" I gasped, quite out of breath.

"Oh, just a conversation with a killer. *Our* killer."

"Hinckley—our killer? But I don't understand . . ."

"My dear fellow, I had assumed you realised immediately that the man we met was not the real Hinckley. No, this fellow—whoever he is—has been following us ever since we left Baker Street. He was sitting in a hansom that had been standing a little way down the road ever since I got up this morning. Must have cost him a pretty penny, since he had no idea when we might be expected to leave.

"He got out of the cab when he saw Lestrade leave, realised we were not with him, then got back in. You'll remember that when we did depart, I insisted on walking a little before I hailed a cab?"

"That's right. I did wonder. You usually insist on getting one right outside the front door."

"That was so that we had occasion to pass his cab and get a look at him. We took him a little by surprise there, I think. He raised a newspaper to hide his face, but not before I'd got a quick look at it and confirmed that he is the man who came into the dining room in Scotland."

"Great Scott, Holmes—are you sure?"

"Reasonably so, old fellow. The man has a distinctive shape to his ears. The lobes are imperforate. I observed it when he passed our table that evening. I commend the study of ears to anyone who wishes to detect crime. No two pairs are quite identical. They mark a man's individuality more clearly than anything else, including his fingerprints. Yes, it's our Scottish friend, right enough."

"But why is he following *us?*"

"To see how much we know, I suspect. So I thought it wise to let him have one end of the thread. When he has one end and we hold the other, it is a moot point as to who is pulling whom.

"You may have wondered why I explained to you in such great detail as we entered the building what we were about to do?"

"Yes, it did occur to me, now you mention it. It's not like you to waste words."

"That was for our friend's benefit. He was

walking just behind us. It was also the reason I took such a tortuous route to reach the department—to give him time to get there first. Which he only just managed to do. I must admit that I was distinctly relieved to hear that noise when we arrived. That told me my supposition was correct and that we were about to meet the ur-Hinckley—the genuine article being temporarily indisposed."

"But wasn't our man taking an awful risk?"

"Not really, Watson—and certainly nothing comparable with the other risks he has been taking lately. It was safe for him to assume that neither of us knew the real Librarian. After all, how often do you pop in for a quick Sanskrit translation?

"No, his impersonation did not lack boldness but in most other respects it was amateurish in the extreme. Even though it was contrived on the spur of the moment, I could have given him so many pointers . . ."

"For instance?"

"For instance . . . if the man you are impersonating habitually wears *pince-nez*, they will leave a discernible indentation on the bridge of his nose. One must either create that same impression with make-up—assuming that you do not wear them yourself—or refrain from removing them, once you have them on.

"That is fundamental but simple. Much harder

to have to fake an expertise you do not possess. The document he claimed to be studying was not Armenian, fifth or any other century. It was clearly written in Aramaic, one of the oldest languages in the Semitic group, and the tongue used by Jesus and his disciples. The merest neophyte student of ancient languages would have known that."

"But what about the Sanskrit—and the book?" I asked. "He seemed to know about that."

"He knows about as much Sanskrit as—Mrs. Hudson," Holmes retorted. "Botany—fiddle-sticks. My own knowledge of the language is by no means extensive but even I know that the inscription says THE BOOK OF KOR. It merely remains to determine precisely what that signifies. Which I propose to do as soon as you have gone."

"Gone? Gone where?"

Holmes pointed in the direction of the room we had just left.

"The Hinckley clone thinks we have bought into his deception. Having given us time to leave the vicinity, he will continue about his business. I wish to know what that business is.

"I want you to follow him, old fellow, and see where he goes—the hunter hunted."

"And you, Holmes?"

"Once you have both departed, I shall rescue the real Hinckley, who, even now is, I suspect, cursing his fate in one of his own cupboards. And from him I hope to learn the meaning of the Book of Kor.

"Listen—I think that is the door opening. I rely on you implicitly, Watson. Happy hunting!"

Before I could say another word he had vanished into the labyrinth of corridors. I had just enough time—and presence of mind—to slip into the next room I found, as the hurrying footsteps of someone I presumed to be "Hinckley" approached.

Safely inside with the door opened a mere crack, I verified his identity as he passed. Gone—as Holmes had predicted—were the wire *pince-nez*. In place of the affable academic was an expression of grim determination and—did I imagine it?—a touch of concern.

Then from behind me a woman's voice enquired—"May I help you, sir?" I turned to find the female equivalent of what I imagined the genuine Hinckley to be, peering at me benignly from behind her desk.

"Ah, thank you, madam," I said and then added the first thing that came into my head. "I was under the impression that this was the Gentlemen's Wash Room but I see I was mistaken. Good day!"

And with that, I was gone.

In the distance, far down the corridor I saw Hinckley turn a corner and, once again, I found myself thinking of the White Rabbit. I set off in pursuit and soon realised the truth of what Holmes had been saying. We were, in reality, quite close to the museum's main entrance. He had led us all around the houses to reach our destination.

When I reached the great doors, Hinckley was descending the wide steps leading to the courtyard and the thoroughfare beyond. Fortunately, the flight was wide enough for me to hasten down one of the sides without his seeing me. As he passed through the iron gates I was close behind him, using a party of tourists to screen me from him, should he decide to turn around. But it clearly never occurred to the follower to think that he might himself be followed.

He raised a hand and whistled to a passing hansom. A moment later it was trotting away in a southerly direction.

As soon as the wheels began to turn, I beckoned to another and jumped in, giving the driver the direction I had always hoped to have the occasion to utter—"Follow that cab!"

On we proceeded at a steady pace. Along Shaftesbury Avenue to Piccadilly Circus, where I fully believe that you really will meet everyone you've ever known, if you stand there long enough.

Over to my left as we turned into Piccadilly itself the Criterion Bar. I recalled, as if it were yesterday, the evening I wandered aimlessly into there, soon after my return from that abortive Afghan War, where I ran into Young Stamford. Hearing of my need to find lodgings I could afford on my niggardly Army pension, he whisked me round to see a friend of his who was desirous of sharing a nice suite of rooms.

By such a casual coincidence was I to meet Sherlock Holmes. Seven years ago—seven years in which so much had happened.

The thought of Holmes brought me back to my present mission.

The cab in front was making good time but seemed in no particular hurry and there was certainly no sign that my quarry had any idea that he was being followed. On the other hand, I had no opportunity to study him, since he had the blinds of the vehicle firmly pulled down—a somewhat strange act in itself, since the day was distinctly overcast.

Now we were circling Hyde Park Corner and bearing left into the maze of streets that lead to Victoria. Was Hinckley—for I could not put another name to him—making for the station as a means of escape? Somehow I thought not. If Holmes's reconstruction of events was correct, the man's mission was far from over. It was much more likely that I was chasing the fox back to his earth.

If so, it was a somewhat luxurious one, for the

cab rolled to a halt outside No. 36 Eaton Square, an imposing residence that had clearly been converted into luxury apartments. From the front door issued a uniformed *concièrge*, who hurried to open the cab door.

I had instructed my own driver to stop several yards further back, so as not to arouse suspicion. As a result, I was unable to hear the exchange of remarks between passenger and *concièrge*, but I gained the distinct impression that the servant was surprised to see Hinckley, even though he obviously recognised him. At one point he looked back at the building he had just left, as though puzzled, then returned to the business of helping Hinckley descend from the cab.

Except that it wasn't *Hinckley* who stepped out of that hansom!

This was a man with a full head of salt-and-pepper hair and beard and moustache to match. He wore spectacles with heavy black frames and, as he moved towards the building, I saw the reason for the *concièrge*'s concern. This man limped slightly. The *concièrge* offered his arm but the limping man brushed it aside somewhat brusquely and hastened up the steps and into the house. The *concièrge* followed more slowly, looking more than a little discomposed.

My mind was in a turmoil. Had I followed the wrong cab? But no, I had made mental notes of certain marks on the back of the vehicle—a trick

I had picked up from Holmes—and this was the hansom Hinckley had hailed outside the British Museum, right enough.

Had I been daydreaming on the journey and failed to notice a substitution of passengers? Possible, I concluded, but highly unlikely. I had been on the *qui vive* ever since I received Holmes's instructions.

So what was the explanation of what I had just witnessed?

The solid sound of the front door being closed told me that one thing was certain. There was nothing more to be gained by waiting here. At least I now had an address that seemed to have something to do with our investigation, if only I knew what.

I instructed my driver to continue on to Baker Street, as I continued to seek an explanation in vain. Then, as we approached the Park, it occurred to me that Holmes would probably be some time about his business at the Museum. I determined to take a turn in the Park and walk the rest of the way home. Accordingly, I had the driver drop me at the nearest gate and set off briskly. Perhaps the fresh air would clear my mind.

At times like this I am inclined to take a fresh look at my fellow men and women. How much we normally take them for granted as part of the scenery, as we pass among them. And yet each of them is an intrinsic part of—wasn't it Balzac who called it the *comédie humaine*? That young soldier over there, walking with his girl . . . that shabby elderly man conversing with himself . . . that respectable pair of matrons walking their dogs . . . each of them has a story, be it a comedy or a tragedy. Or, as is far more often the case, something of a cross between the two.

Saints and sinners rub shoulders with one another and most of them go by us unnoticed until we have need to seek them out—or they make it their business to seek *us* out.

It was at this point in my reverie I became aware that I was myself being followed. For some minutes I had been vaguely aware of the clip-clop of horses' hooves just behind me and I had registered that a cab was about to pass me. Now I realised that it was keeping a discreet distance behind and matching my pace.

My first thought was that my cabby had misunderstood my instructions and had thought I meant him to keep me company, until I decided to ride again.

As I turned to speak to him, I noticed that the driver was a different one from the one I had paid off a short time ago. In fact, the vehicle was not a London cab at all but a smaller carriage with an insignia on its door that was unfamiliar to me.

When he saw me turn in his direction, the

driver increased his horse's pace to draw level with me. He was certainly no ordinary cabbie, for his complexion was dark to the point of being swarthy. It was the kind of face I had seen more often than I cared to remember on the northern front.

Suddenly, the carriage door swung open and a green-gloved hand beckoned to me.

"Please come in, Doctor Watson, I need to speak to you most urgently. I assure you that you will be perfectly safe."

A moment later I was seated inside the carriage staring into the haunted eyes of the Emerald Lady.

The next few minutes were among the most unusual I think I have ever spent in my life. It was as though I had stepped out of modern day London straight into the Arabian Nights. I know I'm mixing up my religions here, but you catch my drift.

To begin with there was that perfume. It was more incense than ordinary perfume. Holmes mentioned it subsequently and he may very well be right—there seemed to be an ingredient in it that affected the senses. I had never been this close to the woman before but somehow she seemed to be out of focus—now closer, now further away. I had trouble concentrating on what she was saying and it was not simply her beauty that distracted me.

For, indeed, she *was* very beautiful. The olive face was a perfect oval and the brown eyes as deep and dark as rock pools. Strange and wonderful beings seemed to dance and spin in their depths, inviting you to join them and yet somehow warning that one did so at one's peril. For this woman was greatly troubled and her fear emanated from her.

You may think me a foolish romantic, but she reminded me of nothing so much as Rider Haggard's great creation, Ayesha—the immortal "She-Who-Must-Be-Obeyed," though I had no sense that there was evil in this woman. I felt no fear of her; merely an inexplicable desire to relieve her fear, if I could.

Somehow she seemed to sense what was going through my mind and it was as though she was giving me time to adjust my thoughts. Finally, she spoke again.

"Doctor Watson, I hope you will forgive this unseemly intrusion but I could think of no other way to communicate with you and Mr. Sherlock Holmes. I beg you to help me. My life is in danger and with it the lives of many of my people, should anything happen to me.

"Even though I am nominally their leader, I am watched day and night. Today I managed to get away for a drive, saying that I needed some air and since Ayub . . ."—she motioned towards the driver sitting up in the front of the carriage—

"is loyal to me, I am safe for the moment. And who knows—perhaps they believe that—

> I am in blood
> Stepp'd in so far, that, should I wade no
>   more,
> Returning were as tedious as go o'er."

Seeing my shocked expression seemed to relieve her tension, for she burst into peals of girlish laughter.

"You are shocked that I should know my *Macbeth*? But you English really are the most contradictory people! You give the world the most sublime thoughts and words and then you are surprised when we foreigners give them back to you! But again, I must apologise, Doctor, for I believe I malign you by calling you 'English' when, in reality, you are Scottish?"

Then she behaved as coquettishly as any schoolgirl.

"In which case, you should appreciate my quoting the 'Scottish play.' "

What a woman of contradictions this was. Nonetheless, the exchange seemed to have effected an intimacy between us, for she relaxed visibly, gave an instruction to the driver in some guttural tongue, and for the next quarter of an hour or so, we drove round and round the park as she told me her story.

• • •

"As you will have surmised, Doctor, I do not come from your world. I was born in a small country squeezed into unrelenting terrain between the northern India border and Tibet. Perhaps because no one wanted it sufficiently, perhaps because my people have always defended their rocky fastness with the utmost ferocity, it has stayed independent and largely unknown.

"If I say the name Zakhistan, I venture to suggest the place does not exactly leap to mind?"

I had to admit that, though the name sounded vaguely familiar and I, as an old Indian Army man prided myself on having knocked around that part of the world pretty well, I couldn't place it and I admitted as much.

"Frankly, Doctor, that has been both the making and the breaking of my country. It is not of this world. It exists in a time warp of many centuries' making.

"The people are poor and superstitious. They pray to the God Kor, who they believe looks over them and has kept them from the invaders who, from time to time over the ages, have come, looked at those mighty cliffs and departed for easier conquests."

"Kor?" I said. "The name is unfamiliar to me, too."

"As, indeed, it should be, for—like so many of the heathen gods the world over—he is a figment

103

of man's imagination. I see that clearly now. But to my people Kor is all-powerful.

"Legend has it that, aeons ago, in a time of great famine the God Kor descended from beyond the stars on the back of a giant silver eagle. Twined around him were two enormous snakes—cobras . . ."

"The twin serpents!" I exclaimed.

"Just so."

It was only then that I realised that the Emerald Lady was wearing long green silk gloves of the kind most Western women would reserve for formal evening wear. She now peeled one of them back and held out her arm for my inspection.

Around her slender wrist was a golden bracelet, wrought to resemble the entwined snakes. Then I remembered how Holmes had detected its telltale imprint on the letter he had received.

She turned her arm to reveal the underside of it. There, tattooed on the inside of her wrist, was a design of what were clearly two King Cobras facing in opposite directions, their fangs bared, ready to strike.

"From that time on—so legend has it—the crops improved, there were no more raiders at our gates and our country found a degree of stability. All of this is recorded by the soothsayers and elders, who embellish the story at every turn.

"Whatever may or may not have happened in those distant times, my people have continued to worship Kor to this day."

"And what happened to Kor—in the legend, I mean?"

"He departed on his eagle, leaving his serpents behind to work his magic. He also left word— or so the elders would have it—that the serpents should be in the care of a High Priestess of their choosing."

"But how could a snake—or even a pair of snakes—do such a thing?"

"Supposedly, on the day of his departure the God Kor ordered that every woman in the kingdom who had borne a girl child on that day bring the baby to him. The children were placed in the House of the Serpents for one hour. Kor ordained that his servants, the serpents, would 'test' the children by biting them. One of the children would not die. That child would then become the High Priestess and rule over the land."

"How fiendish!" I exclaimed. "And what happened?"

"It was as Kor had prophesied. One baby

survived and as High Priestess lived to a great age. Perhaps the serpents' venom in her blood had something to do with it. I have no way of knowing. All I know is that the tradition has persisted to this day. When the High Priestess feels herself to be failing in health, she calls for the ceremony to be repeated. Thus, the successor is chosen and the tradition remains unbroken. Meanwhile, the Grand Vizier deals with the day to day running of the country."

A sudden thought occurred to me.

"But what about the serpents? They are not immortal either."

"They, too, reproduce and from the nest the High Priestess—who may move among them with impunity—selects the two healthiest males. The succession must be ensured—just as it was written in the Book of Kor . . ."

"The Book of Kor?"

"It contains the teachings of the God Kor, written in his own hand and entrusted to the first High Priestess, as soon as she was of age. It contains the secrets of Life and Death and all Wisdom. It is to us as the Old Testament would be to you, were it written by God Himself."

"And where is this book?"

She looked at me sadly and replaced her glove, seeming relieved only when the tattoo was concealed once more. Now she spoke in an even lower voice, as if afraid that she might be overheard even in such secluded circumstances.

"It is because of the Book that we are here, Doctor. But let me tell you the rest of my story, for it is almost finished.

"Some years ago the High Priestess, Ayala, was taken ill and called for the Ceremony of Succession to take place. The girl babies were duly assembled, the 'test' took place and one was chosen . . ."

"*You* were that child!"

"I was that child, Doctor. That is what the tattoo signifies and it will be with me to my dying day. And if you were to look more closely at the design, you would see that what appear to be the eyes of the serpents are, in fact, the puncture marks made by the serpents themselves. They mark my immunity but they also seal my destiny.

"But then a strange thing happened. Ayala— who was not as old as many of her predecessors— recovered her health. I was anointed but not yet needed to fulfill my destiny.

"Then one day an even stranger thing happened. Ayala called a meeting of the elders and told them she had determined our country must learn more about this dangerous and changing world in which we lived. Even though we could keep ourselves apart, we heard disturbing stories from the few traders who crossed our borders. I was to be sent, accompanied by one of the elders—a devious man called Khali—to Europe to be educated in the ways of the great world outside. In due time I would bring that learning back to enrich the people who would by then be my subjects."

"Why, that's amazing," I could not help but exclaim. "How could that primitive woman have such foresight?" Then I realised the implied insult to my companion and stammered to a halt.

It was as though the Emerald Lady read my innermost thoughts, for she reached across and put her tiny gloved hand on my arm.

"It is my eternal good fortune that she did and I shall bless her name forever. Perhaps she had what you in your world would call a 'woman's intuition.' Is that not possible, Doctor? Oh, and Doctor . . ."

"Yes?"

"My name is Uma. I would consider it most pleasing, if you were to call me by it?"

"And my name is John. I would be equally honoured."

And there, in that gently jogging conveyance, the High Priestess of the Serpents and a middle-aged ex-Army doctor formally shook hands. And if I'm honest, I held on to that delicate little hand longer than was strictly necessary.

Finally, Uma sighed but it sounded to my ear to be a sigh of relief and contentment to have told her story so far.

"Well, John," she continued at last, "I came to

Europe on my thirteenth birthday with my *amah* as chaperone and Khali as an attendant. Money was no problem for us, since Zakhistan is rich in precious stones, and in your world money can buy most things, as you know.

"In consequence, I received my education at Roedean and then travelled for spells to Paris and Geneva to those bizarre institutions you call 'finishing schools.' But that was of no concern, for to me *everything* was an education.

"So for the last twelve years I have been one of you, as well as one of them." She shifted her eyes to where the driver sat. "And for all of that time I have known that one day I must return to my country, whether I wanted to or not."

Suddenly she seemed to lose that splendid control and clutched my hand tightly. "And I do *not*—oh, John, *how* I do not!

"But, you see, when I was sent to learn your ways, I was also given a sacred mission to fulfil."

"Mission? What mission?"

"I must find and return the Book of Kor."

"But I thought you said it was your Bible?"

"So it is—but it has been taken from us and my people believe that no good will come to us until it is found. They blame drought, tempest, crop failure, any natural accident—even a sick child or a nagging wife—on its absence."

"Then how was it lost?"

"Some years ago—long before I was born—an

expedition of white men, hunters and scientists mostly, braved the pass and arrived one spring. They were the first white men in many centuries; certainly the first anyone then living had ever set eyes on. And since they brought many toys and magic—which I now know to be rifles and telescopes—they were considered a wonder. Many of these toys, though not the guns, they left behind as presents.

"When they left, my people entertained them to a great feast and waved them farewell. But one of them had in his possession the Book of Kor. How he obtained it is not known to this day, for the holy serpents guard it. But somehow he did and substituted for it another book that looked much the same. It was only when the High Priestess came to consult it for some rare ritual that the substitution was discovered. Since we had no access to the outside world at that time, there the matter rested. But my people have never forgotten and have created for themselves a self-fulfilling prophecy of doom and disaster."

"Now you have discovered its whereabouts?" I asked excitedly. Things were beginning to come together. Wait until Holmes hears about this! Of course, the Book of Kor in the photograph?

Her face suddenly seemed smaller and I could see the child who had been chosen within the woman she had become.

"The tragedy is that we have and we have not.

And yet at the same time we have released a great evil."

Her eyes caught mine and I sensed an inestimable power in their depths.

"Let me explain what brings me here and why I have crossed your path and that of Mr. Holmes.

"Some weeks ago Khali and I received a visit in Paris from one of my countrymen, an emissary from the High Priestess. He bore two messages from her. The first was to say that, now the Great God Kor was finally calling her to join him in Eternity, it was time for me to return to fulfil my destiny . . ."

"And the second?"

"She had received information which would of a certainty lead us to the Book That Was Lost. Some time earlier another white stranger—this one travelling alone—had arrived there, hoping to trade with my people. During his stay he was naturally told the story and shown certain artifacts the earlier party had left behind and many drawings of the Book of Kor. At this he became very excited and claimed that he knew who had the Book. Seeing that riches were there in plenty, he drove a hard bargain.

"He and the High Priestess's emissary were to seek me out in Paris and together we would reclaim the holy Book and bring it back home. There he would receive his due reward.

"In due course, that is precisely what happened—or so it was intended. On his second visit the emissary brought this man with him and the man had a photograph that proved what he said was indeed true."

"What was the man's name?" I asked eagerly.

"When I asked him that, he just laughed and said—'Why not call me Mr. Smith? I have many names but that will do as well as any for an old sinner.' And that is all he would say."

"And the photograph?" But I knew what she would say.

"It was a group of young men. It looked as though they were in some sort of college setting. They were smiling at the camera and the one in the middle was holding a book. Mr. Smith said it was what we were looking for—the lost Book of Kor."

"Did he say anything else about the group?"

"He gave a very unpleasant smile and said it was strange how Fate had a way of delivering one's enemies into one's hands. I didn't know what he meant by that."

But I fancy I do, I thought.

"Oh, and one other thing," she went on. "I forgot to mention that the emissary brought with him the holy serpents. As guardians of the Book, they will know the true book from any fake.

"Mr. Smith said the Book was surely in England and that we should all go there immediately. We rented a house in Regent's Park and had it

112

officially registered as our national Consulate, so that we would be undisturbed."

I thought but did not say that any residence that houses a couple of King Cobras can be reasonably assured of a high degree of privacy.

"And why did the killing start?" I surprised myself by the harsh tone that entered my voice. I must have shocked Uma, too, for she buried her face in her hands and her slight frame was wracked with sobs.

"Mr. Smith insisted that Sunil, the emissary, and I should go with him to see Sir Simon Briggs in Scotland. He said he was merely an intermediary and that Sir Simon would only deal with the principals, should he have the Book. He said Briggs was the logical place to begin, since he was holding the Book in the photograph.

"Then, when we arrived at the inn, he said that Sir Simon refused to see us and that we must take a more direct approach. I see now that it was a lie. I don't believe he ever intended to contact him in a conventional way. The man had something that belonged to us. We were justified in breaking in on him. That was his argument. And I was too weak to argue."

"And so you did?"

"Yes. Smith forced the French window and all three of us entered the house that way. Sir Simon was terribly shocked. Oh, it was horrible!

"Finally, he agreed to look at the photograph

and I believe he was genuinely puzzled. He said he remembered there *was* some old book that was supposedly the Society's Holy Writ—I didn't know what he meant but Smith clearly did. But he said he had no idea what had happened to it when the Society was dissolved. Frankly, I believed him and the only thing I wanted to do was to get out of there.

"But do you know the most peculiar thing of all, John? The most peculiar thing was that I could swear Smith had met Sir Simon before and Sir Simon seemed to find something familiar about Smith. He kept looking at him in a puzzled way, as though he couldn't quite remember something."

"And then what happened?"

"I finally found my courage, apologised to Sir Simon for our intrusion, and insisted to my companions that we leave the way we had come."

Just as Holmes had deduced.

"We had a trap waiting and set off for the inn. But when we had gone a little way, Mr. Smith said he had left something behind and would join us in a few minutes. He got out of the trap and started walking back to the house . . ."

"Where he proceeded to murder Sir Simon by walling him up in his own airtight vault," I interposed.

Her fingers tightened on my arm until her grip became quite painful.

"I *beg* you to believe I had nothing to do with that! When Smith returned to the inn—and you and Mr. Holmes saw him enter—he told us that he had returned to the Library to find that Sir Simon had had a tragic accident and that we should leave immediately before we became caught up in police enquiries. It was only in the next day's newspapers that I read what really happened. And by that time Mr. Smith had spun his filthy web. He told Sunil and I no one would believe we had not been involved in the death. We were at the scene and we had a motive. Who would believe some heathen foreigners?"

"He said that?"

"Those were his very words, John. And, of course, he was right. We *are* heathen foreigners in the eyes of your people."

Now it was my turn to take *her* hand but I could think of nothing to say, for her observation was sadly all too true.

"Mr. Smith said that he intended to fulfil his part of the bargain but now we would do things *his* way. Then he laughed and said something like—'Be sure your sin will find you out.' I wrote it down later, so that I wouldn't forget it."

"*Book of Numbers*. Chapter Thirty-Two. Verse Five," I said automatically. For some reason it is one of the few lines from the Bible that has stuck with me since my scripture class at school.

"So we hurried back to London. By now I was growing very afraid indeed of our 'Mr. Smith.' I was becoming convinced we were dealing with someone insane. He kept humming a little song which ended in the words 'Seven green bottles standing on a wall. And if one green bottle should accidentally fall' . . ."

"It's an old children's nursery rhyme. I sang it myself when I was young."

"And he kept changing his *appearance* . . ."

At this my ears really pricked up.

"How do you mean—changed his appearance?"

"He would brush his hair different ways. Sometimes he would appear with a moustache and sometimes not. He was like an actor trying out different parts. It seemed to amuse him to see my reaction and he would laugh a lot, then suddenly become very serious. When we got back to London, he said he had to see a man about a house and went off singing his little song. But this time the words had changed to—'Six green bottles' . . ."

"I'm afraid he went to see a man in *the* House— the House of Commons. Victor Pelham, M.P."

"You mean that man who died while he was making a speech? Don't tell me he was another of the young men in the picture? Smith would never tell me the names of the others. He said the less I knew the better. But this is terrible, John. *Two* deaths now. The Book of Kor is surely cursed. What are we to do?"

"That, my dear Uma, is what Mr. Holmes and I will decide the moment I apprise him of what you have just told me—which I presume I have your permission to do?"

"Oh, please, John and the sooner the better!"

"I am no legal expert but I believe I am safe in saying that you personally have committed no crime, save the relatively minor one of trespass. Now that you have told me what happened in Scotland, I have little doubt that the authorities would not press charges of being an accessory to murder . . ."

I saw her shudder at the mention of the word.

". . . in any case, as an official representative of your country, you enjoy a high level of diplomatic immunity. My advice would be to return to the Consulate, stay within it as much as possible and keep your eyes and ears open. Where 'Mr. Smith' is concerned, try and pass on to us any information that may present itself. Omit nothing, however apparently trivial. It may be of the utmost importance."

Holmes would have been proud of me, for I was quoting him word for word.

"And now I must hurry back to Baker Street."

With that, I took her hand and kissed it.

"You are a good man, Doctor John Watson," came her voice from the depths of the darkened carriage, as I closed the door behind me. "And may God—yours or mine or whoever there is—go with you until we meet again!"

And as the carriage rolled away, I turned towards Oxford Street and home with a lighter step.

CHAPTER SEVEN

M r. Hinckley—my friend and associate, Doctor Watson."

"Doctor Watson—Mr. Hinckley. And, of course, Inspector Lestrade you know."

I had arrived back at Baker Street bursting with my news and expecting to find Holmes alone. Instead, there seemed to be a room full of people.

Mrs. Hudson was clearing away the tea things—good heavens, had I been gone *that* long? Lestrade was over by the fireplace discreetly brushing cake crumbs from his jacket and Holmes was sprawled in his favourite chair and showing no inclination to rise from it. Instead, he appeared to be enjoying my evident stupefaction as I shook hands with a mousy little man who looked as though he lived in perpetual twilight— which, in a sense, he probably did.

To add to my confusion the little man pumped my hand up and down with surprising strength— gained, I presumed, from carting those heavy dead tomes around all day.

"Delighted, Doctor, delighted to meet Mr. Holmes's *alter ego,* if I may put it so. My, my, such an exciting day! Little did I think when I was drinking the morning cup of tea which my landlady, Miss Lippincott, so kindly prepares

119

for me that I would be the victim of a dastardly attack. One does not expect mindless violence in a department such as mine. Oh, dear me, no. Egyptology, perhaps, in the light of its current and somewhat misplaced vogue . . . And then to be rescued from durance vile by no less a personage than the world famous Mr. Sherlock Holmes . . ."

I thought I saw Holmes raise an eyebrow minutely, though whether the response could be attributed to vanity or irony, it was impossible to tell.

"Oh, I shall have *such* tales to tell at the next meeting of the Curators and Librarians' Association."

There was a warning cough from the direction of the fireplace.

". . . though Mum is, of course, the word for matters which only those of us who are, so to speak, 'in the know'—know."

And he tapped his beaky nose significantly.

Holmes now decided he had played this particular fish long enough to his own amusement.

"As I suspected, Watson, the imposter who took the real Mr. Hinckley by surprise and, only after a fierce struggle . . ."

Hinckley puffed himself up at the recollection of that titanic encounter.

". . . managed to subdue him, held him captive in the store room, where I found and released him shortly after your departure. He was then able to decipher and explain the inscription on the book Briggs was holding in the photograph . . ."

"Oh, you mean the Book of Kor," I offered casually, "the teachings of the Great God Kor, the holiest of relics for the people of Zakhistan?"

There was total silence in the room for all of a minute before Holmes rose from his chair and grasped me by the shoulders.

"Watson, I declare I *never* get your limits. There are unexplored possibilities about you, my dear fellow. Here are we dithering and dickering about with our paltry pieces of eight, when you have obviously unearthed a treasure trove!"

"Oh, I wouldn't go so far as to say that," I said with all the modesty I could summon up. "But I do believe I have both seen and observed a few things since we parted."

And then I told of my encounter with Uma, the Emerald Lady, which provoked—as I knew it would—the immediate response.

"My dear fellow, the fair sex really *is* your department, isn't it?"

To which I felt no need to offer a response.

Holmes was now pacing the room, his brow furrowed in concentration, his hands clasped behind his back. It was an attitude I knew so well.

"Capital, Watson. So now we have breached the enemy camp, though the situation of your Emerald Lady seems parlous, to say the least.

The so-called 'Mr. Smith' is clearly deranged. It is to be hoped that we can bring matters to a speedy conclusion."

At that moment the thin voice of Hinckley piped up.

"The lady's account of the Book of Kor is, indeed, riveting, though incomplete as to certain details. From your account, it would seem that she does not wish to give you an impression that her country remains mired in medieval superstition—

"The legend of the God Kor, for instance, is surrounded in considerable speculation. There are even versions that claim that he was of extra-terrestrial origin and that his golden eagle was some sort of mechanical contrivance that landed there by accident. We moderns, of course, who know that 'flying machines' are a mechanical impossibility, can easily discount such a story.

"However, what can not be gainsaid is the importance the Zakhistanis through the ages have accorded the Book of Kor. So holy is it that they believe that any non-believer who so much as touches it will die. A prophecy they are perfectly prepared to fulfil themselves, should the God not intervene first."

"And so 'Smith'—or whatever his name really is—is using this belief to justify his own independently motivated actions," said Holmes ruminatively. "The God Kor is merely using him as his agent, or so he would have the others believe. 'Accept what I do—or you betray the will of Kor.'

"And talking of his identity, I believe Lestrade has something to offer in that direction, don't you, Lestrade? He was about to reveal it when you made your dramatic entrance, Watson."

Lestrade now moved over to the table and took an envelope from his inside pocket. With magisterial deliberation he removed the contents and laid them out on the table, as if he were a croupier dealing a hand of cards.

"Scotland Yard has managed—using its considerable resources—to track down the aforementioned and elusive Mr. Robert McKay—one of the so-called Seven Sinners. By pursuing a fiscal trail . . ."

"Oh, come along, Lestrade," Holmes interrupted him impatiently, "what have you found out about the fellow?"

Lestrade dropped the formality immediately. I often wonder if this is not his side of the game the two men have fallen into playing with one another.

"He's a rum cove, McKay, by the sounds of it. After that business up at Oxford, he's never seemed to settle anywhere for long. A brilliant academic mind. Written a dozen books. Held a chair at several minor universities—but never for very long at any one place. Restless sort of chap.

Travelled all over the place but particularly in Asia . . ."

"What was his subject?" Holmes asked.

"Oh, I can tell you that," said Hinckley. "If it's the same Robert McKay—which I presume it is—he was for many years one of the leading authorities on ancient anthropology. We have many of his early theses in my department. A brilliant mind, as you say, Inspector. Such a tragedy we have had nothing from his pen these past several years."

Lestrade consulted his notes.

"Quite right, sir. 'Professor of Anthro-po'—what you said. But then, two or three years ago he dropped out of sight, like . . . until just the other day. We have a record of him buying a house in central London—I've got the address 'ere somewhere . . ." He began to consult his papers. "Anyway, we managed to dig up a few photos. They're a year or two old now, mind." And he indicated the table.

As I leaned over to examine them, I heard someone gasp and then realised that it was me.

"But that's *him*," I exclaimed. "That's Hinckley!"

Only then did I remember that, in my excitement at telling them about my encounter with the Emerald Lady and parading my superior knowledge about the Book of Kor, I had completely forgotten to report on my original mission.

I attempted to repair the omission forthwith and told them how I had followed the cab into which I had clearly seen the false Hinckley climb.

"But when it arrived at Eaton Square, it wasn't Hinckley any longer. *This* is the man who got out and went into No. 36!"

"Then we've *got* 'im, Doctor—Mr. 'Olmes. It's as clear as day to me now."

"Then perhaps you will be so kind as to explain it to the rest of us, Lestrade?" said Holmes, settling back into his chair again.

Lestrade was now in full stride.

"McKay falls out with the rest of his Oxford friends, nurses this grudge over the years. He starts to travel to foreign parts, then turns up in this Zakhistan place, where he hears about the Book of Kor and how the locals will do anything to get it back. 'Right,' he says to himself, 'I happen to know where *that* is. I'll get it back for them'—and you can be sure he's getting a fair old reward for doing it—'and I'll get my own back at the same time. What could be neater?'

"Then, when he finds Briggs 'asn't got the book after all, he loses control and kills him. Goes over the edge, like. 'Hello,' he says, 'why not do the same to all of 'em, until I find it? It'll look like the Curse of Kor on the infidels and, in any case, those infidel johnnies are in it up to their necks already, see?' "

"And what about this morning's events,

Lestrade? How do you explain them?" Holmes asked calmly.

The Inspector paused briefly and a frown knitted his brow. Then he plunged on.

" 'E's killed Briggs. Now he tries Pelham but Pelham hasn't got it, either. So he kills Pelham. Oh, and by the way, we checked Pelham's flat. As we thought—torn apart from top to bottom."

He paused dramatically. Holmes motioned to him to continue.

"A fascinating thesis, Lestrade."

"Well, *then* 'e remembers the photograph he left behind all messed up and 'e has another look at it. Now—and here's the nub of the thing, gentlemen—while he meant to point out the *victim* and tell us that a Sinner had met his just desserts, he now notices something else . . ."

"Which was . . . ?"

" 'E notices that this 'ere book, wot got 'im into this business in the first place, is sitting there right smack in the middle of the picture, crying out to be identified by somebody else with the wit to check out what it says on the cover."

"Somebody like you, Lestrade?"

"Well-er—yes. Well—like *us*." And he swept his arm around the room in an all-inclusive gesture. For a moment he looked slightly disconcerted, but then he carried on, swept away by the force of his own narrative.

"You see, gentlemen, by now he knows

something else that is likely to upset 'is apple cart. He knows that Lestrade of Scotland Yard is on the case . . ."

"Not to mention Sherlock Holmes," I couldn't help adding.

"Of course, Doctor, I was just coming to that. *And* Mr. Sherlock Holmes, the well known consulting detective. The power of inductive reason means we're going to track down the meaning of that book.

"So he keeps a careful eye on your movements, Mr. 'Olmes, and this morning, sure enough, he finds you going to the British Museum. Now, is it likely, with everything that's going on, that you and Doctor Watson are spending a quiet morning looking at a lot of mummies? I don't think so.

"Now, he's a smart one, this Mr. McKay, I'll give him that. He guesses where you must be going, gets there ahead of you—and the rest we know. Then, when he thinks he's managed to put you off the scent, so to speak, he hops into a cab, resumes his normal appearance and goes 'ome.

"There, you see, Doctor," he concluded triumphantly, "as I've often heard Mr. 'Olmes himself say—'There are no mysteries, once you know the explanation.' "

And with that he dropped into a chair, looking for all the world like a cat that has had more than its share of cream.

I looked over at Holmes. So often had he brought one of Lestrade's edifices tumbling down with a pointed word or two but on this occasion I saw no sign of dissent. Quite the opposite, in fact.

"Well, Lestrade, you seem to have explained everything. All that remains is for us to go along to Eaton Square—36, I think you said, Watson?—and apprehend Mr. Smith-Hinckley-McKay. Perhaps you would have one of your men call upon my brother, Mycroft, and ask him to meet us there. It seems only fitting that, having been in at the beginning, he should share in the *dénouement*."

Ten minutes later we were in the Inspector's carriage bowling south towards Eaton Place. As we left him at the kerb side, I had the distinct feeling that—despite our effusive thanks—Hinckley was looking a little forlorn, rather like a child seeing the door of the toy shop close in his face. But still, he *would* have a lot to tell the fellow members of the Curators and Librarians' Association.

Nothing disturbed the peace of Eaton Square and I had the distinct impression that nothing ever did. The same well-dressed people got in and out of the same immaculate carriages. The same neat little nannies walked the same shiny perambulators. God was most certainly in his

Heaven and all was right with the world in the immediate vicinity of Eaton Square, S.W.I.

Having said that, I thought I detected a certain diminished *sang froid* on the part of the *concièrge* of No. 36. He greeted us politely enough but looked uneasy, I felt, when Lestrade introduced himself.

"Is there something wrong, Inspector? I assure you that I would be the first to know. This *is* Eaton Square, after all, and . . ."

"That, my good man, is precisely what we are here to find out. I believe you have as one of your tenants a Mr. Robert McKay?"

Now the *concièrge*—who had given his name as Judson—was distinctly worried, although, like any good professional, he attempted to hide it behind a courteous manner.

"Oh, Mr. McKay? Indeed, yes. A very—*private* gentleman, Mr. McKay. In any case, Inspector, I'm afraid you've missed him. He went out some little time ago and it must have been something important, for he was in a great hurry."

"So much so that he didn't even have time to address a word to you?" Holmes enquired.

"As a matter of fact, that's quite right. We always take a moment to exchange pleasantries. We've quite a pride in these little courtesies at 36. Why, I've had tenants say to me . . ."

Whatever the tenants had to say to Mr. Judson we were not to learn, for Lestrade—now with the bit firmly between his teeth—took command of the situation.

"I shall have to ask you to use your key to let us into Mr. McKay's flat, if you please. My colleagues and I are investigating a series of serious crimes and we have reason to believe there may be evidence on the premises. Of course, if you insist on an official warrant, that can be here in a matter of minutes—along with several uniformed constables who will probably traipse up and down Eaton Square for the rest of the day. Still, if your tenants don't mind that . . ."

Judson visibly shuddered. Pulling a bunch of keys from his pocket he led the way up the front steps and into the lobby.

As we did so, a cab pulled up and Mycroft levered his bulk to the pavement, ordering the cabbie to wait.

"A useful trick I learned from our friend, Oscar Wilde," he explained, as he puffed up the steps to join us. "If you find a good cab, keep it all day."

In a few terse sentences Holmes brought his brother up to date.

"I believe I have done justice to your thinking, have I not, Lestrade?"

"Oh, certainly, Mr. 'Olmes." Turning to Mycroft. "Quite obvious, really, when you use what I like to call 'deductive reasoning.'"

"Well, well, McKay, eh?" said Mycroft. "He

always was something of a queer fish, but even so . . ."

Lestrade motioned imperiously to the *concièrge* to lead the way.

Up a grand and sweeping staircase we went, an ill-assorted little group, until on the first floor we came to a solid oak door bearing a highly-polished letter "4." Judson produced a key from his ring and opened the door with the flourish of an impresario presenting an act.

We entered another world.

The room was like another chamber in the British Museum—except this one would have been closed to the general public, for it was a shrine to erotica.

The late afternoon sunlight illuminated carvings and paintings that bore the signs of their different indigenous cultures but otherwise had only one thing in common. They depicted every possible variation of the sexual act and the fact that most of them were exquisitely rendered by craftsmen of no mean skill made them all the more insidious in their appeal. Heaven knows why, but I found myself thinking how grateful I was that my darling Mary was not there to see this lewd display.

" 'L' for Lust."

It was Mycroft putting into words what the rest of us were feeling.

Only Holmes seemed unsurprised by the sight.

While the rest of us stood there transfixed, he examined every corner of the flat—checking the bedroom and bathroom that opened off the main room. He returned to us, shaking his head.

"The bird, I'm afraid, has flown."

Then, turning to Judson, who was rivetted by a bronze of two young men that owed more to Sparta than SW1 . . .

"You have failed to tell us of what transpired here earlier today. I would be grateful if you would relate everything you heard and saw. The slightest detail may be of the utmost importance."

Judson's jaw, which had been slightly ajar from his perusal, now dropped appreciably.

Holmes gave the man no quarter.

"Any *faux* gentility on your part will do nothing to help the people who employ you and may significantly impede the progress of a criminal investigation. Your failure to be entirely and immediately frank with us may well constitute a criminal act in its own right. Isn't that true, Inspector Lestrade?"

"A very *serious* offence," Lestrade chipped in with his best official tone.

"I assure you, gentlemen, I had no intention of withholding information. I was merely concerned with the privacy . . ."

"Of your tenants," I offered. I have learned in working with Holmes in this mood that it often helps if the person being questioned feels that one of us, at least, is sympathetic to his plight. It certainly worked on this occasion.

"Exactly, sir." Judson looked gratefully in my direction. "I thought there was something amiss the moment Mr. McKay arrived back earlier this afternoon. He wasn't himself, if you know what I mean."

"In what way 'not himself'?" Mycroft boomed.

"Brusque, almost rude. Not himself at all. Why, we usually enjoy a few friendly words . . ." Then, seeing Holmes's granite expression—"You see, the strange thing was that when he came in, I thought he was in already," he finished lamely.

Then he remembered something. "And then he started talking to himself . . ."

"What do you mean—*talking* to himself?" Lestrade was looking a little less ebullient than he had when we entered the flat.

"Well, I just happened to overhear as I was going about my duties, you understand. He seemed to be arguing with himself. Naturally, I couldn't hear the actual words . . ."

But not for want of trying, I thought.

". . . and his mood seemed to come and go. At one moment he laughed—a rather unpleasant laugh . . ." His face clouded at the memory. "Then everything went quiet. And a little later, as I told you, I saw the back of him as he went out. And that is positively all I can tell you, gentlemen."

As he had been talking, Holmes had been

pacing around the room and I noticed that he was careful to touch nothing. Suddenly his head snapped in the direction of the unfortunate Judson.

"Who cleans Mr. McKay's rooms?"

"Oh, no one, sir. Mr. McKay is most particular that nothing should be touched and now I can see why. Some of these pieces appear to be most— unique. He made a point when he took the flat that he would look after that aspect of it himself. No one is allowed to enter these rooms. Why, I myself have never seen inside since the day he moved in."

He looked, I thought, a little wistful, as he surveyed the room.

"And yet someone else *has* been in here," said Holmes. "Someone has moved all the larger pieces, as well as the pictures—anything that might contain an aperture . . ."

He did not need to add ". . . that might contain a small book."

". . . and I fail to see why someone who was clearly a perfectionist . . ."

"Oh, *indeed.* Mr. McKay would often say—'A place for everything and everything in its place.' It's a creed I've lived by myself . . ." His voice faded away as he caught Holmes's eye.

". . . would bother to move objects that he had taken great care to arrange in the first place. You see the marks in the dust and the slight scratches where the heavier items were moved in a hurry?"

And, indeed, looking closer where Holmes had indicated, the marks were evident.

"McKay was not talking to himself. There were two men in this room, as is perfectly clear from the indentations in these two armchairs. Men of habit like McKay have a favourite chair and will use no other . . ."

I thought that I could name at least one other person in this room of whom that was also true. Perhaps even two, if I were honest.

"There were two men who argued. One of them left. Which leaves us with one . . ."

"But Mr. 'Olmes," Lestrade objected, "there's nobody in this 'ole flat except us."

Now Judson interrupted excitedly.

"I've just remembered something else. I did hear *one* thing Mr. McKay said. He said—'I think it's time somebody paid a visit to the lady.' Do you think he could have had a woman in here?"

I was surprised that Holmes did not answer at once. Then I saw that he was looking at a large object that dominated one end of the room. I was surprised now that I had not taken more notice of it earlier but the contents of the room were so bizarre that one's visual sense became blurred.

It was made of wood and stood about seven feet high. At first glance I thought it might be an Egyptian mummy case but the surface design was all wrong for that. Although time had faded it, it looked like a primitive depiction of a woman with an enigmatic smile. She stood there with her hands primly folded in front of her but there was something wholly malevolent about her.

I saw that Holmes was now kneeling in front of the object, as if giving obeisance. He put his finger on the richly-patterned carpet, then lifted it for our inspection. It was stained with a drop of blood that the pattern had concealed.

" 'It's time somebody paid a visit to the lady,' I believe you said, Mr. Judson. I might reply— *Cherchez la femme.*' Except I very much fear that we have found the lady in question."

"Of course," Mycroft murmured close to my ear, "an Iron Maiden."

Quietly as he had spoken, his words had carried to Holmes, who rose to his feet and began to examine the object from all angles. He seemed to be speaking to himself, as if reading from one of the volumes in his Index.

"A medieval instrument of torture, fashioned with cruel irony in the shape of a woman by someone who clearly had no love of women. Few escape her close embrace and I fancy this is a case where she has been overly affectionate. Ah!"

He seemed to press something on the side of the casing and slowly the whole front of the accursed thing swung open. There, impaled on the metal spikes that lined the whole contraption, was the man I had seen leave the cab and enter the building earlier that day. Hair, beard, moustache, just as I remembered them.

Holmes was examining the dead man's face minutely, running his fingers along the jaw, as if seeking to find the pulse that was long gone.

Behind me I heard Mycroft reciting under his breath—

"An age in her embraces passed
Would seem a winter's day,
Where life and light with envious haste
Are torn and snatched away.

"Our friend, Pope had a word for every occasion, however lugubrious. Wouldn't you agree, Doctor?"

Before I could answer, there was a loud noise from the doorway that made us both turn in that direction.

The genteel Judson had fainted.

CHAPTER EIGHT

O h, that's the real McKay right enough," said Sherlock Holmes.

We were back in Baker Street with the curtain drawn against the darkening skies that threatened rain—a fitting accompaniment to our collective mood.

Lestrade had been left behind to handle the routine associated with sudden and suspicious death. While he had not been happy to have his pet theories exploded, he was taking solace in doing something with which he was familiar.

"And despite what Lestrade might like to think, I think it highly unlikely that the man committed suicide! For one thing, his hands were tied behind him and there was a gag in his mouth—both of them peculiarly difficult feats for a man to carry out on himself. I have tried more than once in the course of my own experiments."

We were sitting in the half light, nursing well-earned whisky-and-sodas.

Mycroft picked up the conversational ball.

"So presumably what the Doctor saw was our murderer, *disguised* as McKay, entering No. 36, where he argued with him . . ."

"The 'talking to himself' Judson overheard?" I interposed.

"Precisely so. Then overpowered him, searched the flat but again failed to find what he was looking for . . ."

"Then punished the Sinner," Holmes added. "Perhaps you did not get close enough to the body to notice it, but there was a letter 'L' smeared on McKay's forehead in the dust from the room. 'L' for Lust. A title well earned, if that room is any indication of the life he has been leading."

"You know, Holmes, the thing that strikes me is that each of these fellows seems to have adopted one of the sins as some sort of joke to begin with and then grown into it. How do you account for that?"

Holmes smiled a wintry smile.

"Saving your presence, my dear Mycroft, I would venture to guess that somewhere deep in the recesses of the human mind—an area that we have yet to chart—we are all of us yearning to find the part we are destined to play in the human comedy. Without doing so deliberately and perhaps without even fully realising what they were doing, each of them found this charade answered that need for them. Once they had decided that in their different ways, they had no need for the society. Indeed, the last thing any of them would want was to have six other people observing them live out their fantasies."

"And now *one* of those remaining fantasies

involves the deaths of the rest," Mycroft suggested.

"So it would seem," Holmes agreed. "Along the way something has perverted someone's personal fantasy, so that revenge and retribution have become key components of it and the Book of Kor the excuse for his actions."

I had to get it off my chest. "I still don't understand where the Book comes into the murders."

"The Book is merely a symbol to all connected with it. To the Emerald Lady and the simple people of Zakhistan it represents their destiny and their hope for the future. To our disturbed friend the symbolism is quite different. The theft of the Book by the Sinners—as he sees it—must be paid for. Not that he cares a fig for the content of it or its religious significance to others. He has chosen to believe that it is now his mission to retrieve it and punish the original sin of stealing it. It legitimises his own personal motive."

"Briggs, Pelham and now McKay . . ." Mycroft mused. "Which leaves Pascal and—in the absence of Challenger and Summerlee—my good self . . ."

"What about—what's his name?—Staunton? Shouldn't he be on your list?" I asked.

"At this point I don't believe we can afford to leave anyone off our list," said Holmes. "Except you, of course, Mycroft," he added with a brief smile. "Somehow I don't see you donning a false beard in the back of a hansom, then temporarily shedding approximately half of your *avoirdupois* by some sublime act of prestidigitation."

The glance his brother returned to him was opaque to say the least, then the image overwhelmed even Mycroft's innate dignity and he dissolved into a fit of laughter mingled with coughing that left him red-faced. By this time we were all laughing and the tension in the room palpably relaxed.

Holmes went over and stood by the mantelpiece and stared into the empty fireplace, as he reviewed the situation.

"My examination of McKay, cursory though it was, confirmed my belief that he was not the man Watson and I saw in Scotland—the same man who followed us to the Museum. You recall my theory of the individuality of the ear, old fellow?

"Our murderer simply assumed the identity of McKay during the cab ride and did it very well, too. It is a subject in which I have some little expertise myself, as you know . . ."

I remembered Uma's account of the many faces of "Mr. Smith."

Holmes continued—

"He was not his usual friendly self with Judson for the simple reason that, although he could pull off the *look* of McKay, he could not afford to engage in any conversation with our loquacious

Cerberus which would inevitably give him away. That in itself was enough of a clue.

"The result is that we now have three deceased 'innocent' Sinners—with all but one of the rest at possible risk. That one is the murderer himself. And we have seen that the fact that a Sinner does not happen to possess the Book does not save him."

"But surely, Holmes, we only have Staunton to worry about now? Mycroft is safe enough with us watching him and Pascal, Challenger and Summerlee are out of the country and harm's way."

"I think I can add a little something there." Mycroft had recovered his mandarin-like composure. "Just before I received your summons I had been given some further information."

He reached into his jacket pocket and retrieved a handful of papers, several of which could probably change the future of nations. Selecting one, he put on his spectacles and consulted it.

"It would appear that Monsieur Pascal has temporarily deserted his native France for our own shores. There is to be a *Fête Gastronomique* at his West End restaurant, Chez Pascal, tomorrow evening and Pascal himself will be in attendance to prepare with his own hands his *pièce de résistance* dessert, *Surprise Pierre*. He appears to have been here for some days already preparing for it.

"Members of the public are welcome on a first come, first served basis. I think, under the present circumstances, that we may be well advised to be among those who are first to come and even be served."

"And talking of being served . . ." Holmes turned from the fireplace, rubbing his bony hands and with a rare smile on that saturnine face. "I do believe we have earned ourselves a decent dinner this day. Equally, I have little doubt, my dear Watson, that my brother, Mycroft, values our services as his personal Swiss Guards highly enough to insist on paying. So where shall it be, old fellow—Rules or Simpsons? The choice is yours."

Simpsons it was and by the time I sought my bed, relaxed and replete, the long day was beginning to take its toll.

I tried to review the sequence of events and their meaning, as Holmes had taught me to do. It was his habit to rationalise aloud using me as his audience, for it was his contention that it helped him to arrange the facts and to discern the pattern in them. I could also hear him repeat in my mind his mantra—"It is of the highest importance in the art of detection to be able to recognise out of a number of facts which are incidental and which vital, otherwise your energy and attention must be dissipated, instead of concentrated."

So which of the facts *were,* indeed, vital and which incidental?

Three men out of an original seven—no, eight—had been murdered, ostensibly in the quest for the holy Book of Kor. And yet the person charged with the sacred duty of recovering it appeared genuinely horrified by the deaths and I could not find it within me to believe that anyone could counterfeit her degree of revulsion at the acts committed in her name.

Ergo, the Book was the means and not the end, a convenient rationale that excused the murders in some supposedly holy cause and incriminated its followers. A false trail, in fact.

But, if that were the case, the murders of the Sinners were the *real* purpose and why would the murderer stop until he had paid off the debt, as he saw it, owed to him by *all* the other Sinners?

Suppose he found the Book before that aim was wholly accomplished? Would he return it to the Zakhistanis? Or would he perhaps hold on to it, using it as blackmail for their silence and later on, when he was safely away from the long arm of English justice, extort some further fee from these primitive people? The more I considered it, the more persuasive the line of thought became.

Next I considered what Holmes always refers to as "the psychology of the individual." What did we know of the killer?

He was determined and ingenious, one had to give him that. Uma's claim that he could change his appearance at will had been proved tragically correct by our own recent experience. In perpetrating each of the murders he had run considerable risks of being interrupted and caught.

And the murders themselves. Imaginative, if that was the word I wanted. Each of them tailored to suit the individual Sinner's proclivities— Avarice, Pride and Lust—and then signed in a cavalier fashion that was meant to call attention to its perpetrator's ingenuity. But then, the man *was* an Oxford scholar.

Something else occurred to me. It had long been Holmes's contention that a criminal rarely changed his *modus operandi* and that the habitual criminal invariably took greater and greater risks as a way of showing his invincibility.

If that were so in this case, then he would attempt to match any further murders to the sins of the individuals. In the case of Pascal— supposing Pascal was not the murderer—that would involve Gluttony. For Mycroft it would have something to do with Sloth. Staunton? None of the above but, then, we did not know enough about Staunton to associate him with any other specific sin. The Sin of Omission, perhaps.

Logic dictated that it had to be either Pascal or Staunton. Pascal, we now learned, had been in the country at the time of all three murders. Staunton? Again, we knew nothing.

Which left Challenger and Summerlee. Were they really in darkest Africa or had they returned quietly and without fanfare with quite a different mission in mind?

Try as I would, I could not reduce the permutations any further. Perhaps with a good night's sleep, things would seem clearer but somehow I doubted it.

As I drifted off, I recalled something Uma had said about a song. What was it? "Six green bottles . . ." It seemed important but I could not for the life of me imagine why. And then sleep claimed me.

CHAPTER NINE

When I came down the next morning, I found the unmistakable signs that Holmes had already breakfasted and departed. The morning papers were littered around his chair. It is one of his less endearing habits to read them and then cast them aside to fall where they may, whereas civilised human beings who share accommodation with other civilised human beings will have the common courtesy to fold a newspaper, so that someone else is able to read it.

There is one advantage, however, to Holmes's lack of tidiness. It is always obvious what has caught his interest. This morning it was clearly the full page article in the *Telegraph* about Pierre Pascal's *Fête Gastronomique*.

And, if further evidence were needed, he had left one of his Index volumes lying open at the entry on PASCAL.

Guillaume, Pierre's father, it appeared, had been head chef at the court of Napoleon III under whose patronage he had founded the world famous restaurant, Chez Pascal, which his only son, Pierre Aristide, had subsequently inherited. Pierre had opened branches in London, Brussels and Berlin. The entry gave lists of the many awards for *haute cuisine* that both men had won as well as several of their famous recipes, ending with the son's celebrated *Surprise Pierre.*

Assuming that the chef were not our murderer, what *surprise,* I wondered, did somebody out there have in mind for Pierre, Monsieur Glutonnerie?

Set into the piece were photographs of both men. Pierre, I noticed, boasted a luxuriant moustache which dominated the lower half of his face, making it next to impossible to distinguish his features. You might hide *three* murderers behind such a moustache, I thought, as I stroked my own more modest effort.

When I had picked the day's news out of the papers as best I could and satisfied the inner man rather more satisfactorily, I decided to take a stroll. The day was fine and some of the heat that even London experiences in August seemed to have held off.

Without being conscious of having made a decision, I found my footsteps taking me north in the direction of Regent's Park and before long I found myself walking along a stretch of road that contained several minor embassies and consulates.

The houses were all substantial Regency residences, many of them recently converted to this diplomatic purpose. In each case, along this particular street, they were set back from the road at the end of a walled garden, the wall containing a substantial entrance gate.

Suddenly my eye was caught by a brass name plate that looked newer than its neighbours. It bore an all too familiar design and I stopped in my tracks. There were the entwined serpents poised to strike and beneath them the legend—

CONSULATE OF ZAKHISTAN

A gruff young voice behind me said—

"Tell Mr. 'Olmes they're all in there."

I turned, to be confronted by one of the untidiest young urchins one could ever hope to meet and yet, for some reason, I took fresh heart from the sight of that begrimed and freckled face and the sound of that croaking voice, hovering between childhood and adolescence.

"Wiggins!" I cried, "Well met! What are *you* going here?"

It was the unofficial leader of the group of youngsters Holmes had recruited to watch and follow in places where he—or any other adult—would only attract unwanted attention. Holmes declared the Baker Street Irregulars to be as "sharp as needles" and paid them each a shilling a day when they were on a "case," with a guinea going to the lad who found the object of their search. "There's more work to be got out of one of those little beggars," he would often say, "than out of a dozen of the force."

"Keepin' an eye peeled on this 'ere place." His eyes flickered momentarily at the consulate. "Tell Mr. 'Olmes Wiggins will give 'im a full report in due course but right now the green lady's in there, sure enough, and she don't look too 'appy about it. Keeps coming to the winder, until the little brown feller who's 'er assistant or something comes up to 'er and then she moves away again. I'd tell 'im what for, if I was 'er. Well, they're all brown folks in there—except one chap. I've seen 'er arguing with 'im and he stays pretty well away from the winders, as though he oughtn't to be there in the first place.

" 'Ere, Doctor, it'd be best if you was to give me a tanner—no, better make it a bob—just in case anybody's watchin' us. That way they'll just think I'm begging, as usual."

Good old Wiggins, I thought to myself, inventive as ever. If there is any justice—which I am increasingly coming to doubt—you'll end up as Governor of the Bank of England or at least Lord Mayor.

I did as he suggested, deciding a shilling was the safer option. He gave his forelock a desultory tug and was off. I continued my own stroll, for he had made a good point. We did not want to telegraph our own interest in the place. But now we knew where our birds came back to roost.

• • •

When I returned to Baker Street, I passed Mycroft on the stairs and heard him say—"If it becomes absolutely necessary, you have my reluctant consent."

Then, passing me, he raised his hat and said— "I fear that in the past I have used the phrase 'For my sins' too lightly. I now intend to remove it from my vocabulary entirely. Good day, Doctor."

In the sitting room I found Holmes in conclave with Lestrade.

"Ah, Watson, thought we'd lost you. Lestrade, tell Doctor Watson what you were just telling me, if you would be so good."

The Inspector looked a trifle put out.

"I really can't be dealing with these 'ere foreigners, Doctor. I don't know why they can't stay in their own countries, where they belong, instead of coming over 'ere and getting under my feet.

"It's this Pascal feller, or whatever he calls 'imself. I went to see him myself and told 'im we felt he might be in physical danger but not to worry, as we intended to put a guard on 'im night and day while he was in the country. Well, you'd think I'd insulted the honour of *la belle France*! Wouldn't 'ear a word of it. Told me he was a foreign subject and we were lucky to get 'im over here to show us what proper food was all about. Then he went off into some foreign lingo . . ."

"Probably French," Holmes suggested mildly.

"Very probably," Lestrade concurred, totally missing the irony.

"So there we are, Watson. It looks as though we shall just have to take our chances with *cher Pierre*. Incidentally, Lestrade was saying that Pascal keeps a flat above the restaurant for his visits to this country. We shall just have to do our best to keep an eye on the whole building, particularly while the *Fête Gastronomique* is going on."

"Oh, I've got my lads doing that already," said Lestrade, but then a sudden disquieting thought struck him. "But there'll be up to a hundred total strangers milling about the place this evening."

"Nothing, I feel sure, the yeomen of the Yard can't handle," Holmes replied. In the light of recent events I found his confidence strangely unsettling.

Sensing my reaction, he continued—

"We have many options still open to us, old fellow—or, rather, our murderer does and we cannot yet afford to concentrate all our forces on any one of them. Since Pascal seems to be well protected or observed—whichever turns out to be the case—I suggest that you and Lestrade attend this evening's event, while Mycroft and I pursue an alternative course of action."

Although I was uneasy about what my friend proposed, I knew better than to argue with him.

Anything he did was likely to be but one part of some grand plan and he was never happy to reveal that until he considered the moment right.

Consequently, I agreed to meet Lestrade at Chez Pascal a quarter of an hour before the event was due to begin and he departed to inspect his troops.

I then told Holmes of my encounter with Wiggins outside the consulate. What I had to say seemed to please him and his only question was—

"Did you happen to observe, Watson—were there trees in the garden and, if so, how tall were they?"

I told him that, as far as I could recall, all of the houses in that particular row had mature gardens with oak trees of approximately twenty feet in height. Had I known that he was an arborist, I added sarcastically, I would have been sure to take my tape measure along. Not a word of concern about Uma! Sometimes I wonder about the man's priorities.

All of which was apparently lost on him, for all he said was—"Capital, Watson. Well done!" And then he picked up his violin and began to play a cheerful little composition of his own.

Chez Pascal occupied one of those beautiful late 18th century buildings you still find tucked away in a Soho square. As my cab dropped me on the far corner and I crossed the square, a steady stream of people were already making their way towards it.

Pascal was determined to show that he was in town, for he had taken over the whole square for the occasion. A banner proclaiming the FETE GASTRONOMIQUE was suspended from the trees and small booths had been set up in what was normally the communal garden. There Pascal's aproned assistants were handing out samples of various dishes to the passers by. Threading through the crowd were two or three of those violinists and accordion players one never seems able to avoid in Parisian restaurants. I had to admit that it was quite a festive occasion and most—un-English.

With my trained investigator's eye I examined the location. What had Holmes taught me? Try and take in the whole scene objectively, then see if any detail catches your eye and strikes you as discordant in any way.

Virtually impossible to do that here. This was an out of the ordinary occasion, so it was impossible to tell what the square was like on an ordinary day. Here and there among the crowd I thought I could detect Lestrade's men in plain clothes—although to me they seemed to stand out like so many sore thumbs and fingers.

Now I could see what Holmes meant. There

was a pattern to the ebb and flow. For the time being the doors to the main restaurant remained closed to the public and only the uniformed waiters and assistants were allowed in and out. This was what the police were monitoring.

I took a casual stroll through the street behind the restaurant and here the security was even tighter. The restaurant's back doors had been locked and two uniformed officers stood visibly on guard. None shall pass there in a hurry, I thought, and returned to the square somewhat reassured.

Now Pascal's own officials had opened the doors and the crowds were leaving the square and beginning to file inside. There was a cheerful buzz in the air, as they did so. There is nothing an English crowd likes more than something for nothing and to be fed into the bargain.

I was determined to be one of the last to enter, so that I would be able to stand at the back and survey the room. Just as I was making my way to the door, my elbow was taken and Lestrade was at my side.

"Everything's tickety-boo, Doctor. A mouse couldn't get in or out of 'ere without me knowing."

An unfortunate image in the context of a culinary establishment, it occurred to me, but I kept my counsel.

And then, as we entered the restaurant, I saw

them. It was the flash of bright green among the relative drabness of the rest of the people in that room that caught my eye.

There was Uma with—what was the fellow's name?—Khali? Was it my fancy or was she looking more tired and under stress than when I had seen her last? Then, as people often do when they are the object of scrutiny, she saw me, too, and her remarkable eyes flashed a greeting and a warning at the same time.

Just as on the occasion I had first seen her in Scotland, she stood out like a beacon and it was only later that one took in her context, so on this occasion it was only her expression that made me look to the other side of her.

There, sure enough, was the third man from that momentous encounter at the inn. I felt sure that it was only because he was speaking softly into her ear that he failed to notice her instinctive reaction to my presence in the room.

"Mr. Smith" seemed distinctly pleased with himself and what he had to impart but, whatever it was, it made the lady's eyes widen with horror. Her evident distress clearly only increased his pleasure and, when she turned and spoke rapidly and passionately to Khali, the man looked positively smug.

Now he began to survey the crowded restaurant and I quickly averted my gaze and engaged Lestrade in apparently earnest conversation over the menu we had each been given on entering.

"Sandy haired fellow on the left of the woman in green. 'Mr. Smith.' "

"Got 'im, Doctor."

Before we could discuss the situation further, the restaurant's *maître d'* was calling the *mesdames et messieurs* for their attention. He trusted we had enjoyed the *hors d'oeuvres* the staff had prepared for our earlier delectation. And now— in honour of this famous establishment's fiftieth *anniversaire*—he had the honour . . . almost, if one were to permit him the little jest, the *légion d'honneur* . . . to present *le grand maître*, the son of the founder of Chez Pascal—Monsieur Pierre Pascal . . .

As he spoke, I found myself drawn back to "Mr. Smith" and what I saw frightened me, for the man could hardly contain his excitement. And somehow I knew this was not due to the anticipation of the *Surprise Pierre*.

I was looking at the face of murder—or, at least, one of his faces.

And then his expression was wiped clean, as if a damp cloth had been pulled across a blackboard. For through the swing doors behind the *maître d'* swept two minions carrying various culinary implements and in their wake—the moustachioed figure of Pierre Pascal.

Smith's face was now a ghostly white and a vein was throbbing so visibly on his forehead

159

that I could see it distinctly from where I was standing. I nudged Lestrade and nodded my head slightly to direct his attention.

For a moment I though Smith was about to faint. He looked wildly around him, then obviously concluded that he was hemmed in where he stood near to the demonstration table at which Pascal and his retinue had taken their places and would attract too much attention by trying to leave.

Now the great chef went to work. In total silence, like some professional conjuror, he summoned an ingredient from an assistant here, an implement there. His hands were a blur over the large bowl that dominated the table.

The crowd, which had been a buzz of conversation when he entered, had fallen totally silent, too, mesmerised by the man's skill.

Then, with a final flourish, Pascal stepped back from the working surface and spoke for the first time.

"*Voilà. Surprise Pierre!*"

There was a spontaneous outburst of applause from the people in the room.

Now the *mâitre d'* stepped forward once more and raised his hand.

"Monsieur Pascal has requested that one member of the audience should be his—how do you call it?—his *cochon d'Inde*, his 'guinea pig' this evening and approve his concoction before we invite all of you to sample some he has made earlier.

"What about *you,* sir?" And he made unerringly for Smith and pulled him out of the crowd.

Now Smith and Pascal were next to one another and, again I thought the wretched man would collapse.

And then Pascal did the strangest thing. He beckoned to the *màitre d'* to take Smith's right hand and hold it towards him, palm uppermost. Then, taking a device that lay next to the bowl on the table, he proceeded to "pipe" the confection on to the man's outstretched hand.

At which point Smith almost did collapse. By stretching up on tiptoe I could see what the chef had done that caused Smith's reaction.

On the palm of his hand was a swirl of cream in the shape of the letter "G."

The crowd had largely dispersed, puzzled but amused by the incident we had just witnessed. Outside in the square Pascal's handmaidens were serving portions of the famous dessert, which rapidly became the centre of attention.

Within a few minutes Lestrade and I were left alone, wondering what to do next. Then the double doors at the rear opened and Pascal appeared. He stood looking at us and twirling the ends of that magnificent moustache.

And then he spoke.

161

"Come Watson—Lestrade, aren't you going to congratulate me on my performance?"

It was the unmistakable voice of Sherlock Holmes!

Seeing our consternation, he gave one of those sharp barking laughs of his.

"Walk this way, *messieurs*, and all will be revealed."

He led the way through the doors and up a flight of stairs.

Now I could see how he had managed the transformation. As he had often explained, there is usually one main feature that characterises a person. Capture that and few people will look for anything else. In Pascal's case he *was* his moustache; little else of his face was discernible.

He said nothing more but opened a door, indicating that we should enter the room beyond. When we did, I felt just as Alice must have done when she passed through into the Looking-Glass world. For there, sitting on a simple hard-backed chair, with an assistant in close attendance, was another Pierre Pascal!

"Monsieur Pascal, may I present my friend and colleague, Doctor Watson and Inspector Lestrade of Scotland Yard?"

Pascal half rose shakily from his chair and shook our hands. Looking at him more closely, I could see that he was badly shaken by some recent experience. Nonetheless, he appeared determined to tell his story.

"Gentlemen, it is to your friend here that I owe my very life. I was here in my private quarters while my staff were preparing for *la Fête*. I myself had determined to make a small rehearsal for my *grand dessert,* because I had not prepared it for some time. *Surprise Pierre* is not for the *amateur*, my friends . . ."

I looked at Holmes, who shrugged with what for him passes for modesty.

"You must excuse me, but my Oxford English has been—how do you say 'polluted'?—by my native tongue. So—I was absorbed in what I was doing, when the door opened and one of my assistants entered. Or so I thought. I had given strict instructions that I was not to be disturbed but I did not recognise the fellow, although he was wearing our uniform. On these occasions it is necessary to take on extra staff and one cannot remember every face.

"I began to remonstrate with the man, but he closed the door and stood with his back to it. And then he said to me something that really held my attention.

"He said—'You don't remember me, do you, you old sinner?' I looked at him and, in truth, I did not. It was the kind of face that can be any face, you know.

"Then he said—'Just as a matter of interest,

dear boy, I don't suppose you have that old book you chaps used to pore over in the old days?' He could clearly see from my reaction that I had not the faintest idea of what he was talking about.

" 'I thought, not, old sport. You don't mind my asking, I hope? Ah, well, *c'est la vie*, as you Frogs like to say. Or, in your case, *mon vieux*, I very much fear it will be a case of *la mort*.'

"It was then that I noticed he had his hands behind his back. Mine were occupied with my implements, as you may imagine. Suddenly he sprang at me and I saw that he was carrying a length of cord. Before I knew what was happening, he had me bound fast to this chair and my mouth gagged, so that I could not cry out.

"He now appeared very excited and his eyes were shining. 'Are you a religious man, Pierre?' he said. 'I do hope so. In this country there is a proverb—"The greater the sinner, the greater the saint." You should all thank me for making you great saints before your time. My only regret is that none of you will ever understand the greatest irony of all. By dispatching you who once dispatched me, I shall be the Greatest Sinner of you all. But no one will know it.'

"Then he became most angry. 'You ruined my life. My generation discarded me. I carried the mark of failure with me. I made a few little mistakes, perhaps . . .' And now his eyes were mad. '. . . but the business in Calcutta was not my fault and they blamed me for Amsterdam but there were others involved. It was a conspiracy—and it all began with you and your stupid Sinners . . .'

"At that moment he seemed to fight to control himself. 'But all that is in the past now. Now *I* am the winner. I follow *my* destiny, *make* my destiny.' And he laughed a most horrible laugh that I shall remember to the day I die.

"And then . . ."

He stopped and breathed in heavily, as if he were in some pain at the recollection.

"Pray continue, Monsieur Pascal," Holmes urged gently, "your ordeal is almost over."

"Then," the Frenchman continued, "the devil began to feed me my own concoction, my *Surprise Pierre*. He pulled aside the gag and spooned it into my mouth, spoon after spoon. I could do nothing to prevent it and soon I felt myself choking.

" 'The Glutton dies from his own food. I think we might call that his just desserts, don't you, old sport? Don't bother to answer. In this country we are always taught not to speak with one's mouth full.'

"And then a desperate idea came to me," Pascal continued. "I pretended that he had succeeded. I made as loud a noise as I could and slumped forward in my chair against the bonds. He seemed satisfied and just at that moment we

165

heard someone in the next room. He slipped out of the door and just before he closed it, he said—*'Bon appetit, Pierre.'* And then I really did lose consciousness . . ."

He sat back exhausted and his attendant handed him a glass of water.

Holmes moved to his side and put a hand on the Frenchman's shoulder.

"It was not I who saved your life but your own ingenuity."

Then he looked over to where Lestrade and I were standing.

"It seemed to me inevitable that our killer would not be able to ignore such a visible opportunity to add this particular Sinner to his haul . . ."

"But I thought . . ." I interjected.

"That Monsieur Pascal might be our murderer?"

The Frenchman choked over his glass of water.

"Oh, no, my dear fellow, that was never a possibility from the moment we saw the photograph. The ear, Watson—the *ear*. The imperforate lobe. It was always clear that Staunton was our man and the conversation which our friend here has just recounted confirms the man's twisted rationale. A man who is a congenital failure in life—and a potential sociopath into the bargain—has to find someone to blame for that failure. By definition, it cannot be *his* fault.

"Over the years Staunton has decided that

everything that has gone wrong can be traced back to that Oxford rejection—which, in itself, was almost certainly not the first he had experienced. The more he heard of the success of his contemporaries, the greater his resentment grew, until the Book of Kor crossed his twisted path and gave him, in his mind, the perfect excuse. I have no doubt that all of his victims have heard some such rambling diatribe before . . .”

Then, seeing Pascal's obvious distress, he changed his tack.

“I determined that the best way to protect this particular Sinner was to be inside the tent looking out. Consequently, I became one of Monsieur Pascal's supernumerary waiters for the evening—unpaid, I hasten to add—so that I could mingle freely with the crowds.

“This I duly did, until I saw your lady friend arrive, Watson, with her usual retinue. Then I knew I was on the right track. But then—blind beetle that I was—I lost sight of 'Mr. Smith' or Staunton, as we might as well now call him.

“Once I had assured myself that he was not among those present, I realised that, although Lestrade here had the outer perimeter guarded, the inner defences were perilously thin. If *I* could wander at will, so could our murderer.

“I hastened back stage, as it were, and had my worst fears confirmed. Discarded on the upstairs landing was a waiter's white jacket identical to the one I myself was wearing. Staunton had devised the same strategy as had I.

"Luckily, I heard a noise from this room and arrived to find Pascal here *in extremis*. Fortunately, old fellow, I have picked up a smattering of medical knowledge from you over the years and, having torn off the gag, I was able—by employing what I believe is called the Heimlich Manoeuvre—to, shall we say, ease the situation. In doing so, I made one other vital discovery . . ."

"Which was?"

"I discovered that his magnificent facial accompaniment was not, in fact, his. May I . . . ?"

And with that he reached across to Pascal and carefully removed the moustache from his upper lip. Now Holmes was the only Pascal in the room, if you follow me.

The clean shaven Pascal gave a shy smile.

"I suppose when I was a Sinner, I should have taken 'V' for Vanity, if there had been such a thing. I was still a young man when I inherited the company from my most distinguished father. It seemed to me that a moustache would add to my gravitas—you say 'gravitas'? And since I was impatient, I could not wait to *grow* one. So . . ."

"It was Pascal's little affectation that gave me the idea," Holmes added, "an idea that may prove to be the turning point in this little affair.

"I had no doubt that Staunton would wait to see the outcome of his actions. Suppose he were to see a dead man come to life? Would that not cause him to question what he had hitherto seen as his success? And might the fact that he had, in his terms, failed yet again cause him to lose his nerve and give us the initiative? It is, as Shakespeare says, 'a resolution devoutly to be wished' and I fancy we have just gained it, gentlemen."

"There's one thing that still puzzles me," Lestrade interrupted. " 'Ow did you manage to make that Surprise stuff—begging your pardon, Mr. Pascal?"

"Why, I read *Monsieur* Pascal's recipe, of course, which was elegant in its simplicity. Too many of our native cooks, I regret to say, are inclined to present their work as something out of the black arts."

"Black, as in burnt," I sniffed in support.

"And so," Holmes concluded, "armed with Monsieur Pascal's recipe, spare moustache and moral support, I sallied forth to make my debut as a *Maître de Cuisine*—with the result you saw a few minutes ago.

"Incidentally, I would not recommend you to try *Surprise Sherlock*. I have to admit that there appears to be a certain *je ne sais quoi* that eludes the recipe.

"And now, Watson, after all this *haute cuisine*,

I think perhaps we might take ourselves off to partake of Mrs. Hudson's rather plainer English fare. Lestrade, if you would care to join us . . . ?"

An hour later we were doing just that.

CHAPTER TEN

The beast is abroad and you are its only remaining prey."

"And what do you propose I should do about it?"

"I think you must prepare to die!"

The exchange was between Holmes and Mycroft and it left me aghast. Surely Holmes could not mean what I had just heard him say with my own ears?

It was the following morning and we were in Mycroft's rooms in Pall Mall, just across from the Diogenes Club.

Holmes had related the events of the previous evening to the accompaniment of an occasional grunt from his brother. His only question had been about Pascal's plans.

"He showed—quite understandably, I would say—no further inclination to remain in England's green and pleasant land and so Lestrade's men have given him an escort to put him on the next packet from Folkstone," Holmes reported. "But at least he had recovered his sense of humour. He told me to tell you that he did not believe that the worst excesses of the French Revolution could be any worse than what he had been through and he would be sure to invite you round for a special meal he would cook himself when he returned. He said, Senior Sinners should stick together."

That prospect, at least, seemed to arouse a spark of interest.

"In any case, if my sense of Staunton's psychology is correct, then Pascal is now safe from him. He will not wish to revisit the scene of one of his failures.

"Which leaves only you, my dear brother. It leaves you and a man whose demons will now drive him to make up for yesterday's humiliation. He will come, make no mistake about it. The only question is—as *whom?*"

The room fell silent, as each of us considered the implications of what Holmes had just said. Of course, it made perfect sense. Staunton was clearly insane and the logic of the situation would be of no concern to him. If he could reach one man in the wilds of Scotland and another in the privileged chambers of Westminster, he could attempt anything.

And Holmes had put his finger on something else. Whereas the man had presumably approached his first two victims in his own persona, he had assumed another guise with McKay and yet another with Pascal. From now on virtually anybody might be "Mr. Smith."

"Undoubtedly you have a plan?" This from Mycroft.

"Indeed. Would you care to hear it? I'm afraid it will mean that for a day or two Her Majesty's ship of state will have to manage as best it may without your hand on the tiller."

"Before you continue, Sherlock, there is one other piece of intelligence you may care to factor into your plans. I heard earlier this morning that Challenger is expected back in England somewhat earlier from his wanderings. Now where did I put that paper?"

He rummaged among a sheaf of memoranda and I was struck—not for the first time—by the contrast between the brothers in certain areas. Those two great minds missed nothing but organised themselves so differently.

Had we been in Baker Street, the memo would undoubtedly have been transfixed to the mantelpiece—along with his unanswered correspondence—by a dagger. In Mycroft's case the papers were neatly squared and held down by a weighty tome which, as he moved it, I saw was Macaulay's *Lays of Ancient Rome*.

Having found the paper he was seeking, Mycroft scrutinised it.

"Ah, here we are . . . Professor Challenger's boat arrives in Southampton on—September 3rd. And today is—let me see . . ."

"August the twenty-first," I chipped in.

"Which gives us just about enough time for what I have in mind," said Holmes decisively.

"Which is . . . ?"

"Watson, do you remember the little episode which, if I remember rightly, you chronicled as 'The Dying Detective'? 1887 or 8, if memory serves."

"Do I, indeed! Second only to the Reichenbach business, it threatened to bring these grey hairs of mine with sorrow to the grave, as the Good Book says."

Holmes took up the narrative.

"I was attempting to trap a particular nefarious but extremely clever fellow called Culverton Smith, who was using his knowledge of tropical diseases for his own hideous purposes. By pretending to have contracted a rare disease myself . . ."

"The symptoms of which were all too realistic," I felt obliged to add.

"And all due to the art of makeup—which meant that I could not afford to have my old friend and medico get too close. Something for which it took him some time to forgive me . . ." And he gave a brief smile in my direction.

"But, as I say, it was enough to lure Culverton Smith to my parlour, convince him that I was dying, and coax a confession out of him in front of a witness."

"Ah, I *thought* the case seemed familiar. One of your finest tales, Doctor. If I remember, *you* were the witness, hidden behind the invalid's bed?"

"Indeed, I was," I replied, "and I have no intention of repeating the experience."

"Nor will you need to, old fellow. This time it will be my turn to do the honours.

"Friend Staunton has a finely developed sense of the dramatic. The Sinner's fate must fit the 'sin.' Therefore, Mycroft, your 'death' must be related to Sloth. Purely for the purposes of dramatic consistency, you understand?"

"Hm," was the only response.

"We shall let it be known that you have contracted a rare form of narcolepsy. Perhaps you can help us out here, Watson, with a few exotic details . . . ?"

"Well," I said, pleased to be able to talk for once from one of my areas of genuine expertise. "We might go for the variation known as cataplexy. The sleepiness is often accompanied by quite severe hallucinations. Rather like the condition you feigned Holmes, with all your gibberish about oysters taking over the world."

He laughed at the memory but then returned to the matter at hand.

"You may be sure Staunton will be watching carefully for any weak point. He wouldn't be afraid to tackle you in Whitehall or at the Diogenes but, then, you will be at neither."

"Oh, and where *shall* I be?"

"Right here. Confined to your own rooms by your mystery illness. An unconfirmed rumour

175

of your indisposition will appear in tomorrow's newspapers. I have taken the liberty of passing it on—entirely confidentially, of course—to certain journalists of my acquaintance . . ."

"Thank you for your concern," said Mycroft with heavy irony.

"Don't mention it," his brother replied. "Two days later there will be an inter-office memo. Strictly classified, of course, but that, too, will find its way to the gentlemen of the Press."

"And then?"

"And then we sit back and wait for our friend to call."

"And what am I supposed to do, pray, to occupy my time as *le malade imaginaire*?"

"Oh, I think a little Macaulay should pass the time adequately," said Holmes, picking up the sturdy volume and weighing it in his hand. "I seem to remember some of those Ancient Roman doings made rather racy reading."

For the next few days Mycroft—admittedly, with rather ill grace—confined himself to his quarters. Then being a creature of habit whose life ran on pre-determined rails, he adapted to his new circumstances and even declared that he was grateful for the chance to catch up on his reading. He waxed lyrical—for him—one evening on the merits of Suetonius and Pliny the Younger as bedtime reading but I had the distinct impression that my lower limb was being pulled.

Holmes and I would visit him after dark, entering by the rear of the building, after carefully scouting the area in advance. I think it amused Mycroft to see us having to share his isolation but after the first visit, I detected something else. These two brothers had lived parallel lives. Never had they had an opportunity like this to really get to know one another—and they were enjoying it in their own strange way!

The fact that their intimacy essentially excluded me did not bother me in the least. I enjoyed being the sole spectator at their mental and verbal tennis match, as a thought would wing its way over the net, only to be spun back like lightning. It was a rare and privileged spectacle.

On the fourth day Holmes judged that it was now time to create the make-up of advancing illness.

He applied a little vaseline to the "patient's" forehead, some rouge on the cheek bones to create a cadaverous look, a crust of beeswax round the lips to make them dry and finally, a few drops of belladonna in the eyes. In a short space of time the normally robust Mycroft seemed, to all intents and purposes, to be at death's door.

During the daytime Mycroft was "looked after" by a male nurse—in reality a bodyguard—an ex-boxer Holmes had used for what I believe is called "muscle" on other cases that required it.

As night fell he would make his visible departure.

It was Holmes's supposition that Staunton would probably make his move in darkness and so we took to spending ours in Mycroft's spare room, taking it in turn to keep watch with the door ajar.

After two fruitless nights of this, however, Holmes began to be restless.

"We are running out of time, gentlemen," he said to the two of us. "Three days from now Challenger will be arriving in this country and it is only a matter of when the Press pick up that story. Once they do, Staunton's attention will be divided and that we cannot afford. We must bait our trap afresh. One thing our friend will not want is for Sloth to die of natural causes."

In the next morning's *Telegraph* the following item duly appeared—

WHITEHALL GURU SINKING

Telegraph Exclusive
"Informed Whitehall sources (who wish to remain anonymous) confirm to our reporter that Mycroft Holmes, older and only brother of the famous consulting detective, Mr. Sherlock Holmes, lies in a serious and deteriorating condition in his bachelor rooms.

Mr. Holmes contracted a mysterious and

debilitating disease just over a week ago, which has stubbornly refused to respond to the most advanced medical treatment.

Mr. Holmes's long and distinguished service to Her Majesty's Government . . . etc. . . . etc."

It made disturbing reading and a look at Mycroft's convincing make-up made it seem all too likely.

From now on Holmes insisted that we keep our vigil round the clock and he had taken to coming and going quite openly through the front door.

"After all, what would be more natural than an only and grieving brother attending on his ailing sibling?"

To which Mycroft replied—only half-jokingly, I felt—

"Sherlock, I want your solemn word that, when this affair is safely behind us, you will not visit me for the next year. Unless, of course, I really *am* on my death bed."

On the morning of August 28th it was my turn to be on guard duty, for we were now on round the clock alert. Holmes had finally been persuaded to stretch his legs and go for a stroll in nearby St. James's Park.

Mycroft in full ghastly make-up was lying in bed, a book on ecclesiastical architecture on his knee. Thorogood, the nurse/bodyguard and

I were studying that morning's *Sporting Life* and debating our predictions for the day's race meetings, for we were both men of the turf.

At which point there was a sharp rap on the door, which drew all our attention. Holmes had no need to knock and we were not expecting anyone. Besides, Mycroft's rooms were on an upper floor, so that a visitor would normally have to ring the front door bell to gain admittance.

Putting my finger to my lips, I tiptoed into the adjacent room, leaving the door open the merest crack. Before doing so, I silently motioned to Thorogood to see who was there.

From my point of vantage I could not see the door that led to the landing, but only hear the conversation, as the bodyguard carefully opened it.

"Oh, good afternoon, my good man. I am Dr. Silverstone. I believe you were expecting me?"

"Doctor?" Thorogood sounded puzzled. "No, we weren't expecting no doctor."

"How very annoying. I received a request— an instruction, really—from the Prime Minister's office to attend Mr. Mycroft Holmes as a matter of considerable urgency and now you tell me you are not expecting me. And here have I left a Harley Street waiting room full of patients. It really is most irritating."

As he spoke, he moved further into the room and now I could see him. Of middle height with sleekly-brushed silver hair and a neat moustache and small goatee beard to match. He also wore immaculate morning dress—every inch the Harley Street consultant.

"Ah, Mr. Holmes, I presume. My card . . ."

He made as if to reach into an inside pocket and then two things happened simultaneously.

I found myself looking at his ears. And there they were—the imperforate lobes. Staunton!

And then the man—instead of producing a visiting card—spun round in one of those moves Holmes has demonstrated to me from the martial art of *baritsu* and with the edge of his hand delivered a vicious blow to the side of Thorogood's neck. The large man fell as if pole-axed.

Then Staunton, rubbing his hand with the other, moved slowly over to the side of Mycroft's bed. For a moment I could see the "patient" and his performance was every bit as convincing as Holmes's had been those years ago.

He lay back on his plumped up pillows, his eyes scarcely open. The pallor on his face was deathly and his breathing laboured.

"Who are you? What do you want?" he wheezed.

"Oh, you know me well enough, my slothful friend, if you think back to the days of your golden youth . . . your privileged youth . . ."

And he peeled off the beard and moustache.

Mycroft managed to convey a dawning recognition before Staunton moved closer and obscured my view of the bed.

Staunton sounded pleased that he had been recognised.

"Yes, that's right—Evan Staunton, lackey to the great and good. 'Staunton, bring the drinks!' 'Staunton, take the photograph. These mechanical things are beyond me. You're the sort of chap who'd understand them.' And did you think I wasn't aware of all that?

"That's been the story of my life—until now. But once you wipe out sin, you can make a clean start. Did you know that, Lord Sloth? My, but that's a good one. I must remember that. If you'd ever taken a title, it should have been Lord Sloth of Sleep. But now I'm afraid you never will, dear boy. Isn't that what you always used to call me—'Dear boy'?"

While he was talking I pulled my service revolver carefully from my pocket. I have learned never to embark on one of Holmes's escapades without it, for an Eley's No. 2 is a very persuasive fellow in a tight spot. As quietly as possible, I thumbed back the safety catch.

Now I could see that Staunton was picking up a spare pillow from the bottom of the bed and taking his time about it. He was intending to smother Mycroft and send him to an eternal sleep.

Mycroft was now in a genuine dilemma and his response was sheer genius. He began to hallucinate, as I had told him victims of cataplexy frequently did.

"Who are you? Oh, you must be the man from the library. You've come for the book. Surely the libraries are full of books. Why do you need mine? I'll drown *my* book. But no, a good book is the precious life-blood of a master spirit. Be thou a spirit of health or goblin damned? Rest, rest perturbed spirit. But the book, the book! A book of wine, a flask of verse and thou. No, no—a jug of gin, a gin of jug . . ."

His ramblings clearly disconcerted Staunton for a moment. Then he snarled.

"Even at the last you use the words of other men. Well then—'Oh, what a noble mind is here o'erthrown.' The Book is nothing to me now—only to those peasants. And you of all of them would never have kept it. But if you will have it so—then the Curse of Kor be on you!"

As he raised the pillow in both hands, I threw open the bedroom door.

"You can put that down, Staunton. The game is over!"

At that precise moment Holmes burst through the flat's front door.

Staunton whirled around, first in this direction, then that, like a cornered rat. His lips were pulled back from his teeth in the travesty of a smile and he made a sound that was more like a serpent's hiss.

"There's no way out, Staunton," Holmes said quietly.

But for once my friend was wrong. Staunton's eyes went to the window to the street a floor below. Three rapid steps and he threw himself bodily through it with a tremendous crash of breaking glass and splintering wood.

Despite my surprise, I managed to loose off a single shot and I was pretty sure I managed to hit him.

There was a moment of frozen silence in the room and then Holmes and I were at what was left of the window looking down. The rooms were at the back of the house overlooking a communal garden. Below us were fragments of wood and glass and I thought I saw traces of blood. But the garden was empty.

Behind us we heard Mycroft say—

"I can only hope that Her Majesty's Government will see its way to replacing my window or I really *shall* die—of pneumonia. And now, may I *please* remove this ridiculous make-up?"

CHAPTER ELEVEN

N ot, perhaps, our finest hour, old fellow."
It was the following day and we were sitting
in our familiar chairs on either side of the empty
fireplace, having dined on a meal of which Mrs.
Hudson had been especially proud.

As she served us the roast grouse with all the
trimmings, she mentioned something that had
obviously been long on her mind.

"Mr. Holmes, you were once heard to say that
with regard to breakfast I had as good an idea as
any Scotchwoman. Well, I think I can beat any
of them at their own game. Any fool can shoot
one of these wee birds but it takes a Sassenach to
cook it properly."

And with those words she left us to enjoy her
efforts, which were, indeed, excellent, though
I thought Holmes made too much of a point of
picking out the occasional shot and depositing it
ostentatiously on the side of his plate.

Once Mrs. Hudson had cleared the table,
appearing satisfied that we had done justice to
her "experiment," Holmes and I sought our chairs
and our pipes and there we sat, like bookends, I
suppose, staring into the empty fireplace.

I cannot vouch for what thoughts were going
through his head but I know I was reliving those

moments in Mycroft's room and wondering what I might have done differently and whether it was my fault that the whole sorry business had not ended there and then.

"Do not reproach yourself, old fellow. No one could have done more and many would have done a lot less."

"But how . . . ?"

I should have known better than to ask.

"Gazing into that fireplace is like going into a trance, as I know so well myself. Without realising it, your hand steals to the pocket where you keep your service revolver. Then you steal a glance towards my bedroom door and you see yourself once again on guard peering in to Mycroft's room. Now your eyes move to the window as Staunton leaps through it. My dear old fellow, it is not hard to piece the story together.

"But I say again, we must not reproach ourselves for the day's events. We prepared it and our quarry took the bait. What he then did was improbable but not impossible. And he bears our mark—which will enrage that tormented ego even more, for in his own esteem—which is all that matters to him—he is once again teetering on the brink of failure. And we have caused it. Or, rather, in his mind *I* have caused it with my meddling ways."

"So what do we do now?"

At that moment the front door bell rang.

"As to that, I believe we are about to receive some indication," Holmes replied. "According to the vocabulary of the bell, that is the ring of a woman in severe need of advice but one who does not know whether she will be welcome. Tense but hesitant.

"And now, Watson, perhaps I may prevail upon you to let me have some of your Arcadia mixture. Unless, of course, you would prefer me to use the detritus of yesterday's pipe—or is it the day before's? I seem to have lost track of time in all the recent excitement . . ."

Since anything was preferable to the noxious fumes of his stale shag tobacco, I quickly passed him my pouch and, as I was in the act of doing so, there was a light tap on the door, which opened to reveal the Emerald Lady.

Except that this time she was swathed from head to foot in a black evening cloak complete with hood, which she had pulled tight about her face, so that only her large, liquid eyes were visible. And what tormented eyes they were!

Although she had never been introduced to Holmes, it was to him that she addressed herself and I felt an inexplicable twinge of jealousy.

"Mr. Holmes, this madness must cease! My people may be locked into their medieval superstitious beliefs but I have been in your world long enough to know that this is not the way things should be. This man—Smith or whatever his name is—is using us for his own devilish reasons—I see that now. He holds Khali and the others at the Consulate in thrall and plays on their fears of the wrath of Kor."

Holmes leaned forward and fixed her with his calm, penetrating gaze. It worked as I have seen it do so often.

"The beast is wounded, is he not? Therefore, he is mortal and can be dispatched. Tell us what has transpired today."

Uma relaxed visibly. She threw back her hood and her raven hair—which hitherto I had only seen tightly coiled about her head—cascaded around her face, giving her the appearance of a beautiful innocent child.

"Forgive me, gentlemen. I am behaving like a foolish woman and it is the thing I hate most in others."

She drew her cloak more tightly around her and sat back in her chair. I swear that no one—except perhaps *the* woman—has ever made our old basket chair look more like a queen's throne. Once again I thought how she was just as I had always envisioned She-Who-Must-Be-Obeyed.

"I have come to ask for your help, Mr. Holmes. And yours, too, John . . ."

Holmes's eyes flickered in my direction for the briefest of glances but he might as well have said—*"John?"*

"Even though the beliefs of my poor people

are foolish and childlike, they have their dignity and this man—this vile, unspeakable man— is bringing dishonour down upon them. What must I do to stop him? I will do anything, Mr. Holmes, even if my own life is forfeit as a result. It is as nothing to me, after what he has done by involving us in his wickedness."

Holmes leaned forward in his chair and tapped his pipe out in the empty grate. He made a point of not looking at her, as he said—

"You say you would do anything. Even if it meant the end of Kor?"

Now it was Uma's turn to lean forward. Her body was tense and her face mere inches from Holmes's. He had no alternative but to meet her gaze and I knew that what he saw there convinced him.

"We all know that Kor is but a figure of myth," she said quietly. "People need to believe in something or somebody greater than themselves and the legend of Kor answered that need for a backward people, as similar figures have done for other cultures in other times and no doubt will again. But those other races were open to the wider world and the myths vanished. It is time for us to join that world. I see that now so clearly. But how—*how?*"

And she slumped back, exhausted. Gone was the regal figure. In her place was a little girl close to tears.

At such moments Holmes was at his best. His manner immediately became brisk and businesslike. His very tone of voice caused Uma to straighten up in her chair.

"If you will follow what I say in every detail, I promise you this curse will be lifted from you and your people—or my name is not Sherlock Holmes . . ."

"And mine John Watson!"

"Staunton believes he has the whip hand because you are aware of his misdeeds and, by saying nothing, seem to condone them. In this he is playing on what he assumes to be your ignorance of British law.

"In fact, as diplomats of a foreign power you are under no obligation to report what is mere supposition—something which a skilled lawyer would demolish in court as heresay in two seconds. You yourself have committed no crime—merely the folly of believing that the word of an apparent English gentleman was implicitly to be believed.

"Staunton, by his cynical manipulation of what he takes to be your innocence and ignorance, has kept you on the end of his string. But, my dear lady . . ."

And she did indeed look like a dear lady as her eyes brightened at his words.

". . . a piece of string has *two* ends. And if my stratagem works, he will be as tied to you as you are presently tied to him. And we can reel him in."

"Then what am I to do, Mr. Holmes?"

"Precisely what you are doing at the moment. Waiting and watching and playing the part of the frightened young woman. And I use the word 'part' advisedly, for I have rarely seen such genuine courage in someone so young."

"Amen to that!" I added fervently.

"Meanwhile," my friend continued, "the greatest service you can perform for all of us is to continue to let Staunton believe that nothing has changed, that his home base, at least, is secure. I assume he is staying at the Consulate?"

She nodded miserably. "I did not know how to prevent it."

"Which means that he cannot be taken by Lestrade while he is there," I interjected. "The house is technically on foreign soil."

Then Holmes seemed to go off at a tangent.

"I want you to describe to me in detail the layout of the main reception room and its relation to the rest of the house and grounds."

Although she looked slightly surprised at his request, Uma did as he asked, while Holmes took copious notes and even drew a rough diagram at which she nodded her approval.

Then he asked something even stranger to my ears.

"And the holy serpents—are they in good health?"

"They are kept in a special cage and Khali himself feeds them—I was about to say religiously—every day. Why do you ask?"

"Merely to suggest that you refrain from feeding them for the next few days. Make whatever excuse you think fit to Khali. Can you do that?"

"Why, yes. He will obey the word of the High Priestess designate without question. But why . . . ?"

"It may save the lives of many," was Holmes's simple answer. "And now, my dear lady, may I suggest that you return to your post, for all of us have much to do before we can rest easy in our beds. Nonetheless, I promise you there is light at the end of the tunnel. Watson, would you be so good . . . ?"

As I escorted Uma down the stairs, she stopped me in the hallway.

"Tell me, John, does he mean what he says? How can he be so sure?"

"I have never known him promise what he did not think he could deliver," I said with honest conviction, though for the life of me I could not fathom what Holmes was about.

When I had placed her safely in her carriage and seen her on her way, I returned upstairs in thoughtful mood to find Holmes curiously cheerful for someone who had seemingly promised the impossible.

"What do I intend to do, old fellow?" he said, anticipating my question. "Staunton set out to find the Book of Kor. We shall find it for him."

For the next twenty-four hours I saw little of my friend, except on the rare occasions he came back for a brief refreshment and to pore over the stream of telegrams that kept arriving for him.

When the mood is upon him, Holmes uses the telegram as though it were running water. Her Majesty's Post Office need never worry about its solvency while there are criminals abroad and Sherlock Holmes to track them down.

That evening—having not the slightest idea of Holmes's movements or intentions—I decided to dine at my club and enjoyed a most convivial evening. I find it does me good to get back into the real world every now and then after the chaos of Baker Street—an ordered world where a yarn or a game of billiards with a chum is the predictable height of excitement and brutal baffling murders are virtually unknown and strictly against club rules.

Several of the fellows, knowing of my association with Holmes, came over to say how relieved they were that Mycroft had pulled through his recent illness.

Old Archie Sennott put it best, I thought.

"Sticky wicket for our side if Mycroft had been caught and bowled. Straight bat. Nobody better."

Then for some reason or other we got to talking about India. Archie had been up in the north about the same time as I had, although we'd never met.

It turned out—something I'd never known before—that when it was all over, he'd pottered about a bit to see more of the country and had ended up right on the border with Tibet.

"Amazing part of the world, amazing. Places up there nobody's ever heard of . . ."

This was too good an opportunity to miss.

"Ever come across a little place called Zakhistan?" I asked innocently.

And then the flood gates opened. When Archie's had his quota—which he had this evening—it's only a question of what the topic will happen to be when the needle on the record gets stuck.

Tonight it was Zakhistan and although I happened to know that much of what he said was inaccurate, it was still interesting to have some of the details of Uma's story confirmed from another source. Then, just when I was thinking I had heard all that was remotely useful for our present purpose, he said one thing that made all the rambling and repetition worthwhile.

"Well, if you really want to know about those strange little blighters, the man you should really talk to is Challenger. His old man was one of the first white men to get in there. Years ago now, of course. And I hear he had to get out a lot faster than he got in. Quite a stink about it at the time. Forget the details now . . ."

So it was with cheerful tread that I climbed the fourteen steps to our rooms in Baker Street later that evening. Watson, the man who sees *and* observes, listens and learns, sifting the facts and missing nothing.

From above I could hear the strains of Holmes's Stradivarius. The *barcarolle* from *The Tales of Hoffman*, if I was not mistaken—a sure sign that he had had a successful day. It was when I heard Wagnerian scratchings and wailings that I was inclined to make straight for my room.

"Holmes," I said, as I entered the room, "I have good news to report."

"So have I," he replied. "Careful, old fellow you're about to sit on it."

From an ungainly half sitting position I managed to retrieve a brown paper package that was on my chair. I looked at Holmes, who nodded for me to open it. The knots in the string that held it together were not too tight and I soon had it open.

In my hands was . . .

"The Book of Kor!"

"Not *the* Book, Watson—but most certainly *a* Book of Kor and a good enough fake to deceive the most rabid Zakhistani for, if I remember rightly, the only person permitted to actually handle it is the High Priestess herself and the current incumbent is several thousand miles away."

I examined the volume carefully. If it was a fake, it was brilliantly done. The leather cover was worn and stained, as if with much use, and the paper brittle and flaking at the edges of the pages. Seeing me shake my head in admiration, Holmes went on—

"The work of Isaac Goetz, an antiquarian bookseller in Hackney and an old friend of many years' standing. You remember the day of my return from Reichenbach . . . ?"

How could I ever forget seeing the man I knew to be dead standing before me in my own consulting room?

". . . I had disguised myself as a disreputable old bookseller who wished to interest you in his rare collection. Those books, at least, were the genuine article, loaned to me—somewhat nervously, I must admit—by my old friend Goetz.

"He was the only man I knew who could manufacture such a thing at all, let alone in such a short time. I watched him at work today. Watson, I felt humble. There is genius all around us and in the most unexpected places. The paper and ink are of the period of the original . . ."

"But the content?"

"Ah, there we must take our chances, I fear, since we have no idea what the original contained. However, I am reasonably confident that it will pass muster for the purpose I have in mind."

I knew better than to enquire what that purpose might be. He would tell me when he was good and ready and not a moment before.

I then recounted my conversation with Sennott at the club.

Holmes looked pensive.

"Well done, Watson. You have just put the last piece of the puzzle in place and confirmed what my own researches indicate.

"In 1859 the Schumacher Expedition— made up of scientists and explorers of several nationalities—spent several months in Nepal and Tibet. In the accounts published on their return, there is some mention of a splinter group that made off on their own. No details are given but one gains the distinct impression from the way it is written that something went badly awry, for the whole expedition was cut short and returned to England several weeks earlier than planned.

"And there was one other interesting fact buried among the small print . . ."

"Which was?"

"The leader of the splinter group was one Edmund Challenger—Professor Challenger's father."

"Good heavens, so *he* was the one who stole the Book in the first place?"

"So it would appear. And tomorrow we can ask the one man who may have had the key to this whole business all along. You and I and Mycroft will meet Professor Challenger's train at Waterloo tomorrow at 2:15."

CHAPTER TWELVE

Waterloo Station bore all the markings of the battlefield from which it took its name when Holmes, Mycroft and I arrived there the following afternoon.

As luck would have it, Challenger's train had arrived a little early and we needed no Arrivals Board to direct us to the relevant platform.

Platform 7 looked more like a rugger scrum than its usual orderly concourse of travellers and, as the crowd surged to and fro, I was reminded of the days when I used to play for Blackheath myself and would think nothing of piling into such a *melée* of bodies.

Then I saw that there was an eye to this storm. A furled umbrella was being raised and waved about in an agitated manner and a singular voice could be heard over the din of the train whistles and escaping steam.

"Idiots! Nincompoops! I'll sue every last one of your editors. How *dare* you question the veracity of George Edward Challenger?"

Mycroft and Holmes exchanged glances and wry smiles.

"We appear to be in the right place," said Holmes.

"It beggars belief to think there could be *two* of him," Mycroft replied.

Before we left for the station I had studied the entry for this clearly unrepentant Sinner in Holmes's Index. It read—

CHALLENGER,
PROF. GEORGE EDWARD

Educated at Largs Academy, Edinburgh; Edinburgh Univ. followed by post-graduate course at Christ Church College, Oxford . . . winner of Crayston Medal for Zoological Research . . . holder of various prestigious offices in departments of anthropology, from all of which he either resigned or was fired in acrimonious fashion . . . endless other academic awards and learned publications—"Some Observations Upon a Series of Kaimuck Skulls"; "Outlines of Vertebrate Evolution," etc., etc. *Recreations:* Walking, Alpine climbing. *Address:* Enmore Park, Kensington, W.

To which Holmes had added a handwritten note to the effect that Challenger must hold some sort of record in terms of police court fines for assaulting members of the Press who asked him questions he found offensive.

"Ah, well," Mycroft sighed, "I suppose we'd better bail George out one more time or Staunton will find him by the sheer decibel level alone."

With Mycroft's bulk as the point of it, the three of us formed a human wedge and forced our way through the crowd.

At the heart of it stood three bewildered porters, their trolleys piled high with Challenger's assorted crates and portmanteaux, and a ring of journalists, all of them keeping a wary distance—except for one who was on his hands and knees striving to find the pieces of his broken camera. Standing over him, his umbrella poised like the sword of Damocles, stood Professor Challenger.

The first thing that struck me about the man was the contrast between his imposing presence and his physical size. Listening to his bull-like roar from a distance, I had deduced that he must be huge but now I saw that he was a foreshortened Hercules, for he stood well below my height, and I am not a tall man.

But what he lacked in height, he more than compensated for in breadth and, presumably, brain. The spread of his shoulders taxed the limits of his jacket, as did the barrel of a chest.

The head was perhaps the largest I have ever seen on a man and again I was reminded of a bull, for he had the face and beard I have only ever seen in pictures of Assyrian bulls. His complexion was florid—I might say, choleric—

and the beard, which was spade-shaped and extended well down his massive chest, was so jet black that, when it caught the light, it almost seemed to have hints of blue in it.

The brow was equally impressive from what I could see of it under his panama hat. The eyes—when they had ceased to flash fire—would be blue-grey under those beetling black brows and would miss nothing and trust no one.

Finally, there were the hands. Large enough to rival a navvy's and covered with long black hair, they gripped the umbrella with unequivocal menace.

All in all, Professor George Edward Challenger looked more like one of the primates he had undoubtedly been studying in the back of beyond than one of the most highly qualified academics of his generation.

"We seem to be in the right place," said Holmes.

"I hardly think there can be *two* of them," Mycroft replied

And this was the man we were counting on to resolve our dilemma!

If he was surprised to see Mycroft, he showed no sign of it, merely observing—

"Ah, Her Majesty's Government have sent you to welcome me home, have they, Holmes? Perfectly appropriate, too. And who are these people? Minor civil servants of some sort, I suppose. Perhaps they can take care of the luggage?"

Introductions were duly effected, though there was a saurian glint deep in Challenger's eye that told me he knew perfectly well who we were.

"Consulting detective, eh? What sort of job is that, pray? Sounds more like some quack who overcharges you for telling you you've got a headache you told *him* about in the first place. And you, Mycroft. Always thought you could have added up to something more than a glorified office boy, if only you could have been bothered to stir your stumps."

With that last he went too far. For the next two minutes the voluble Professor was rendered mute, as Mycroft—giving us a rare glimpse of what made him central to affairs of state—told him, in a tone that brooked no interruption, what had happened in his absence and why we were here.

"And so, my dear George, you would do us all a great favour if you would, for one brief and shining hour, set aside your natural tendency towards the theatrical and come with us."

Although he had come in like the proverbial lion, Challenger allowed himself to be led out like a veritable lamb. There was the quality of the basilisk in Mycroft's expression that said enough was enough.

Even the Professor's admonishments to the porters attempting to maneouvre his luggage on to their trolleys was positively mild for him—

"I hope you realise you are not delivering coal but handling unique artefacts that will revolutionise all our present theories of evolution!"

Our little party reached the station entrance, where, I was amused to see, Mycroft had once again had his cab wait upon him. Seeing my quizzical expression, his face for the briefest of moments transformed itself into a creditable impersonation of Oscar Wilde and then returned to its normal enigmatic expression.

"My dear Doctor, I have long since learned that a good idea does not mind *who* has it—or, indeed, how often."

Now Holmes was whistling up another cab and directing the winded porters to pile Challenger's luggage into it. As he watched them at work, the Professor asked in a dangerously mild tone—

"Since I am obviously to be kidnapped, am I allowed to enquire where you are taking me?"

Then, with a glance at Mycroft—"Is it the Tower of London for my heretical views on the origin of species? Or for calling the President of the Zoological Society an underdeveloped primate in print? Pray tell."

By way of answer Holmes instructed the driver of the lead cab—

"Enmore Gardens, Kensington, driver. We are taking you home, Professor Challenger. You see, we want to borrow a book."

The room was exactly what one might have expected if a stage designer had set out to create the study of an eccentric professor for a West End play. Books and papers were piled on every available surface and in several cases had begun to cascade on to the somewhat threadbare carpet. Shelves were littered with strange fragments of bones and other, less savoury objects which defied immediate identification. The walls were crowded with a variety of framed diplomas and certificates attesting to the Professor's pre-eminence in this field or that and a virtual gallery of photographs in which Challenger, invariably centre stage, adopted the identical self-satisfied pose.

The light from the large bay window illuminated the myriad dust motes that hung in the air and every time an object was moved, a myriad more rose to join them. It was clear that Mrs. Challenger and her maid were forbidden to disturb this holy of holies on pain of death, although the rest of the house that we had seen as we entered shone like a new pin and it was quite apparent where his domain ended and hers began.

"My dear wife is always telling me that this or that terrible catastrophe is about to engulf me 'for my sins,' but I doubt that even she—the romantic that she is—could have envisaged such poetic justice."

Challenger stroked his great beard thoughtfully and his eyes looked over our heads, as Holmes—with occasional interpolations from Mycroft—gave him a detailed account of the events of the last few days.

"Well, Holmes . . ." Then he paused thoughtfully. "The fact of there now being *two* of you called Holmes forces me to change the habit of a lifetime and call you 'Mycroft.' I have always deplored this modern habit of over-familiarity, but I suppose needs must. This man Staunton has much to answer for."

Then the old Challenger returned momentarily.

"Did I not warn the rest of you at the time I was foolish enough to indulge in that undergraduate nonsense that the man was a charlatan and a poseur? But would you listen? Not one of you!"

He banged on the table in his shabby sitting room in annoyance, causing several objects to fall to the floor. The noise caused the door to open and his wife—a diminutive but fierce little woman—to put her head around it and fix him with a lion-tamer's glare.

"George!"

"Yes, my dear," he replied meekly and the door closed again behind her.

"Gentlemen," he went on in a nearly normal

tone, "I seem to have been in the wrong place at the wrong time. Here you have been having all the excitement, while I have been incarcerated in the wilds with that fool Summerlee, questioning my every move. Naturally, I validated my theories in short order and headed for home. But—can you credit it?—Summerlee refused to join me and insists on retracing every step of our journey to find the mistake he is convinced I made. Pah!"

He paused and a wistful expression crossed his face.

"Nonetheless, I must confess that I rather wish he were here now. It would give me such pleasure to see Envy written across those dessicated features of his when he realised that I, George Edward Challenger, was able in an instant to solve a problem that had beaten the combined and—perhaps one might surmise—possibly over-vaunted intellects of the brothers Holmes."

"Perhaps you would care to elucidate, Challenger—or may I call you 'George'?" Mycroft enquired with dangerous calm.

"I'd prefer Challenger, if you don't mind," the Professor replied totally missing the irony. He was now in full spate.

"Frankly, gentlemen, what is so special about this business of deduction? What else do you think scientists like myself do in our daily work? Come, Mr. Holmes, let me put you to the test.

What, sitting here, can you tell about me?"

I felt my irritation towards the man begin to abate and I smiled inwardly. Little did he know the trap he had just sprung for himself.

My friend pursed his lips and said mildly—

"I dare say you are quite right, Professor. Having only just met you, I can tell very little about you, other than the fact that you have recently started to become vain about your personal appearance, dressed this morning in rather a hurry, were in the habit of smoking a cheroot made of Turkish tobacco in a distinctly unorthodox fashion but have recently given up the habit—presumably at your wife's insistence. Oh, and you had a small dog of which you were inordinately fond but which died while you were abroad. Other than that—and what may be gleaned from reading your newspaper cuttings, I know—as you rightly say—nothing about you."

I was pleased to note that Challenger now wore that familiar glazed expression that was a hallmark of Holmes's subjects.

"Pardon me," said Holmes, leaning across the Professor's desk and gently removing a hair from the arm of his jacket. "The dog was a Jack Russell terrier."

There was a moment's silence and then Holmes put the man out of his misery.

"I am always telling Watson that I shall sink whatever reputation I possess by explaining my little parlour tricks but on this occasion I can see that it is necessary . . .

"Your personal appearance presents no problem. You have naturally strong hair that goes its own way but recently you have detected a bald spot on the crown and attempted to brush your hair over it. It has, however, resisted your best, if intermittent, efforts and thus draws attention to what you wish to conceal.

"This morning you dressed on the ship and—without your wife to check your appearance before you appeared in public—you put on odd socks. I noticed them at the station and since you are not a man to make a deliberately *outré* fashion statement . . .

"When we entered your house a few minutes ago, your wife studied your right hand most carefully—presumably to see if the stains on the fingers that distinguish an inveterate smoker were in fresh evidence, thus proving that, *in absentio* you had broken your promise.

"I use the word 'unorthodox' because, while most of us hold a cigarette or cigar between the index and second fingers, the stains indicate that you are accustomed to hold it between the second and third fingers.

" 'Turkish'? Watson will tell you that I have learned to distinguish between the ashes of some one hundred and forty different tobaccos—I have even written a small monograph on the subject.

"This . . ."—and he picked up a pinch of cold ash from an ashtray on the desk—"though some months old is clearly of Turkish origin." He dropped it back where he found it. "A man remains true to his smoking habits. I see no reason to suppose you have changed yours.

"The dog? Here I fear I tread on sensitive ground. I perceive that you and Mrs. Challenger are a childless couple. Yet you, Professor, are proud of your family heritage and equally proud of your own accomplishments . . ."—and he indicated the gallery of framed photographs with a sweep of his hand. "It is, therefore, inconceivable that you would not include a picture of yourself as proud parents. You do, however, have a record of yourselves with a series of small dogs . . ." And here he reached out and turned around a cabinet photograph of the Challengers holding a dachshund that had been facing the Professor, so that we could all see it.

"When a pet dog and its owner form a bond and the owner is indulgent, as you are, it is not uncommon for the dog to insist on sitting on its master's lap when he is working at his desk. The hair in the cradle of your arm tells its own story. Sadly, the fact that the dog was not there to greet you on your arrival—and the look that passed between you and your wife—tells another.

"I rest my case."

There was a moment's silence before a subdued Challenger said—

"Mr. Holmes, I hope G.E.C. is a big enough man to apologise. You fully deserve your reputation."

He stretched his powerful right hand across the desk. Solemnly Holmes shook it.

"And now," said Challenger, "allow me to make my small but not insignificant contribution to this bizarre tale.

"When we embarked upon that ridiculous Sinners charade and somebody—I seem to remember it was Pelham—said that every half-way respectable society had to have a mystical Book of Rules, I suddenly remembered a whole pile of junk my father had accumulated from his travels. He was, as you may know, a distinguished explorer and scientist in his own right with a reputation not far below my own present one.

"Since he was out of the country at the time, I had no trouble in finding something suitable looking. I had not the faintest idea what it was. A Sanskrit inscription, of course, but that particular field of study has never attracted me and still does not. The others seemed to find it acceptable but then little things please little minds . . ."

"But what happened to it when the Society disbanded?" Holmes asked. Even he, I noticed, was comparatively subdued in Challenger's emotional presence. The man's life force was such that he seemed to suck the air from the room around him. I have never experienced anything quite like it.

"Oh, I put it back with my father's other paraphernalia. He never even noticed it was gone."

"And where is that paraphernalia now?" Mycroft asked urgently.

Challenger looked at him as if he were a dense pupil at one of his lectures.

"Where it belongs, obviously. In the British Museum. The Rare Manuscripts Department. I placed all of his papers there immediately after his death."

"But—" I looked helplessly at Holmes but he gave me a sign to let Challenger continue uninterrupted.

"I have, of course, given those incompetent bureaucrats strict instructions that the Challenger Collection should remain inviolate until I have time to collate it personally—which looks increasingly unlikely—or until after my own death. At which time I have suggested that a complete suite of rooms be dedicated to our memory and achievements. 'The Challenger Annexe' would be perfectly appropriate."

"So the blessed book was under our noses all the time, Holmes?" I could not help but interject.

"So it would seem, old fellow."

And then he explained the whole episode to the

Professor, which amused him immensely. The beard rose and fell on the massive chest as he laughed. Who is acting like the schoolboy now? I thought.

"So now the Great God Kor has *two* books to his name?" he gasped when he had contained his amusement. "And what do you propose to do now, Mr. Sherlock Holmes?"

"I propose to offer one of them to Mr. Geoffrey Staunton—the 'New Testament' to be precise."

There was a stunned silence in the room after Holmes had spoken.

"You mean that after all we have gone through, you intend to let the fellow win, Holmes?"

"Not at all, Watson. Merely that we use *our* 'Book' to entice the rat from his lair. At this very moment he is lurking there, licking his wounds, desperate to avenge himself for what he undoubtedly sees as his humiliation at our hands.

"We must also assume that he now knows that Challenger here has returned. Therefore, left to his own devices, he will make the Professor his next target . . ."

Once more the chest was puffed out and the eyes glared fire. This time I was put in mind of an angry pouter pigeon.

"If George Edward Challenger cannot defend himself against a little pipsqueak like Staunton, then . . ."

Holmes ignored the interruption.

"However, before he has the opportunity to do so, we shall make him *our* target, using the Professor as our bait . . ."

"Bait!" roared that worthy.

"Believe me, Professor, it is a role which will require both courage and unusual subtlety."

"Then I am your man," replied the Professor, somewhat mollified.

"I imagine that financing one of your expeditions must be a tedious and time-consuming business?" Holmes asked in an apparent *non sequitur*.

"Why, yes, tedious in the extreme. But what . . . ?"

"Tomorrow's papers will contain an announcement that you are to hold an auction of a number of your personal and professional effects to raise money for your forthcoming expedition to—where shall we say?"

Now the Professor's eyes really did light up with an almost religious fervour.

"What an excellent idea, Mr. Holmes. I have no doubt that a grateful public would be prepared to pay substantial amounts of money for the most trivial of my surplus items—what my dear wife likes to refer to as 'my old rubbish.' And now that you mention it, I have long had it in mind to pursue the persistent rumours that have come to my ears of a strange plateau that exists deep in the Brazilian rain forests. The stories refer to it as a 'lost world.' Who knows what rare life forms may linger there. Why . . ."

I caught Holmes's eye. No wonder this man's fevered imagination got him into so much controversy. A lost world, indeed! He had been reading too much of that Jules Verne fellow.

"Splendid," said Holmes, as he got up, rubbing his bony hands in satisfaction. "If you will make a list of the items for sale—it scarcely matters what—I will arrange for the auction to take place in the main lounge of the Savoy Hotel two days from now and place an announcement accordingly. I shall also have a personal invitation hand delivered to Mr. Geoffrey Staunton, care of the Zakhistan Consulate, telling him that he will find something to his advantage, should he choose to attend. If I understand his psychology adequately, even though he scents danger, he will be unable to refuse. He will see it as his chance to redeem himself.

"And now, Professor, we will leave you to your unpacking."

As we left, we could hear the piping treble and the booming base notes; the Challengers picking up their perpetual duet of harmonious disagreement.

"What do you make of the fellow, Holmes?"

"I am inclined to the view that, if *anyone* can find a lost world, he can . . ."

CHAPTER THIRTEEN

The next morning I slept late for me and when I came down to breakfast, it was obvious that the day was already well advanced for Holmes.

He was in the middle of briefing young Wiggins who, on seeing me, snapped off his version of a military salute. He has grown accustomed to the thought that it pleases me and, to tell the truth, he is not entirely wrong.

Holmes, who fails to see the need for such niceties, rapidly pulled him back to the business at hand.

"I want you to take this letter round to the Zakhistan Consulate and make sure that you leave it where it cannot be missed. No one is to see you. However, should you be detected, you are to say . . ."

"I know the drill by now, Mr. 'Olmes. I tell them a bloke gave me a tanner to deliver it. Never seen 'im before in me life."

Holmes gave an approving nod, Wiggins a further salute and the door closed behind him. I could hardly fail to notice that, although he had mentioned one letter, Holmes had, in fact, handed the lad two. But I knew better than to question my friend when he was laying the details of one of his *dénouements*.

As I sat down to the boiled eggs Mrs. Hudson had put in front of me, Holmes tossed the morning's *Telegraph* in my general direction. It was folded in such a way as to show a fair-sized display advertisement—

GRAND AUCTION!

PROFESSOR CHALLENGER TO SELL VARIOUS PERSONAL ARTEFACTS AND MEMENTOES TO HELP FUND LATEST HISTORY-MAKING EXPEDITION.

I thought I knew whose hand had penned that last phrase.

It then went on to list the various categories of objects that would be for sale—relics of various primitive cultures, photographs, books, copies of monographs that Professor Challenger would be happy to sign personally. Happy to? Let someone try and stop him, I thought.

FROM TIMBUCTOO TO TIBET . . .
NOW YOU CAN SHARE THE FANTASTIC VOYAGES OF THIS GREAT MAN!

The advertisement ended with the details of time and place the following evening.

"If that does not coax our friend out into the open, my name is not Sherlock Holmes," said Holmes, re-reading it over my shoulder. "He will hope to find the Book, fulfill his commitment to his heathen employers, if for no other reason than that he has boasted he can do so . . . and then go after Challenger."

"And what happens when he realises that the book is not *the* Book?"

"By that time the trap will have been sprung, old fellow."

And he would say no more.

I had my own business to attend to for much of the rest of the day, although I would, of course, have given it up willingly, had Holmes required me to. Irritatingly, he did not and on the occasions I was in Baker Street, I had to content myself with watching a succession of messengers coming and going about their inscrutable business.

Finally, as dusk was beginning to fall, Holmes seemed content with his day's work.

Indicating our favourite chairs, he crossed the room, took down my pouch of Arcadia mixture from the mantelpiece, and brought it over to me in one of those rare but thoughtful gestures of his that acknowledges—without the need for words—his understanding of my frustration at being left out of events.

When we had our respective pipes going, the introspective Holmes emerged.

"You know, old fellow, I sometimes think that the human mind is a bottomless pool into which we dive at our peril. We look at someone—even someone we think we know well—and on the surface all appears calm. And then one day—for reasons we may never fathom—down in the deep something stirs.

"In the case of friend Staunton that something is unspeakably evil and primeval. Slowly but implacably it rises, until it hovers near the surface waiting its moment.

"Staunton's beast first took shape in adolescence, a compound of the fears and perceived inadequacies that beset him. It fed on every defeat and rejection, real or imagined, until it was stronger than he. But still it slumbered.

"Then one day, years later and by a coincidental combination of circumstances—if, indeed, one is inclined to believe in coincidence—it is goaded into life. And now someone must pay, for now the beast must feed."

"But how has this 'beast,' as you call it, survived all these years?" I interjected.

"Simple. It has fed on Staunton. And now it *is* Staunton. The young man Mycroft and his Oxford friends knew was probably no more than a callow fellow overshadowed by cleverer but not necessarily superior minds. But with the cruelty of youth they were—at least in part—responsible for creating this, their own nemesis. And somewhere, even now, comparable unwitting tragedies are in the making, tragedies we are powerless to detect until the beast emerges from the depths."

"So Staunton is doomed?"

"There *is* no Staunton. Only the beast and the beast must be taken. Believe me, Watson, I take no pleasure in this case. It has the elements of Greek tragedy—pity, terror, *catharsis* even. My only satisfaction is that I have been able to act as my brother's keeper and perhaps repay him in some small way for watching over me during the Reichenbach affair."

He looked thoughtfully at the mantelpiece, where some time ago he had propped a small framed etching of the infamous Reichenbach Falls. The very mention of the place conjured up sobering memories for both of us and for some moments we sat there in silence.

Eventually, Holmes spoke again.

"Do you know what should give us the greatest pause, old friend?"

"No, what is that?"

"Mycroft and his friends were arrogant and thoughtless but not deliberately malicious and yet they conspired to help create their own destruction. What new leviathans are we creating by *our* incursions into the lives of others?

"We are divers in deep waters, Watson. Never forget that. Divers in deep waters.

"And now I suggest we shake off these morbid thoughts. I happened to notice the De Reskes are singing tonight. Let us have glorious harmony tonight before tomorrow's inevitable discord. What do you say?"

CHAPTER FOURTEEN

The Savoy Hotel descends gently from the main entrance just off The Strand in a series of almost imperceptible layers until it reaches its riverside exit. At the heart of it lies the main Lounge and it was in that direction that the crowds were making their way, as I entered the building a few minutes before seven, when the auction was supposed to start.

I was not, I must admit, in the best of tempers. As I had been dressing to come here, Mrs. Hudson had delivered a note from Holmes, whom I had assumed was doing the same. It was one of his typically cryptic missives—

"Dear Watson,
   The game's afoot!
   I shall be at The Savoy at 7:00.
   As always, your role in tonight's drama will be critical.
   Do not fail to bring your other faithful friend!
   Remember the deep waters
                    SHERLOCK HOLMES"

That was all very well, but how was I to know what my role was supposed to be? No doubt he would deign to tell me when we met at the auction.

As I crossed the Lobby, my eye was caught by a large poster which featured a photograph of Challenger in heroic pose over the legend—THE GREAT CHALLENGER COLLECTION! The same motif adorned the cover of the catalogue I was handed as I descended the steps to the Lounge. For something I knew to have been printed in a hurry, it was rather an impressive piece of work. Having agreed to co-operate, Challenger had clearly entered into the spirit of the thing and his hand was everywhere apparent in the printed descriptions of the various "lots."

"Unique collection of Arawak Indian blowpipes assembled during my epic expedition up the Orinoco in 1887. Item 5 was obtained as a result of hand-to-hand combat with the leader of the tribe, a singularly vicious fellow. Full details will be found in my book, *River of Death: A South American Odyssey*, signed copies of which are available."

The room was filling up as the hour approached and I looked around for Holmes without success. What did catch my eye, however, was the looming figure of Mycroft, trying to look as unobtrusive as possible behind a pillar at the back of the room. I made my way through the crowd and joined him. As he saw me, he produced a piece of paper from his pocket and raised an inquiring eyebrow. I nodded. So we were *both* under starter's orders.

There was a sharp rap on a gavel and the crowd began to settle. Now I could see that there was a small platform against one wall of this large, mainly open space and on it was an auctioneer's lectern. Behind it stood Challenger himself. He had clearly decided to be his own auctioneer.

Now he began to lay out the rules of engagement, so to speak. We were all of us fortunate to be here today to so much as lay our eyes on the fruits of a career—a career, he might add, of unparalleled achievement, which history would undoubtedly . . . At this point one of the audience—almost certainly a journalist—asked him to "Get on with it!" Challenger turned on him a withering gaze and informed us all that anyone who interrupted the proceedings by a coarse remark or a frivolous bid would be ejected from the building by him personally and he ventured to speculate that many of his audience today knew that he was perfectly capable of carrying out his threat. He would now begin the auction.

I scanned the room again. No Holmes. No Staunton either, as far as I could see. And then Mycroft nudged me. Pretending to consult his catalogue, his eyes flickered towards the far corner of the room, where a swarthy Indian man had just entered.

"The ears have it, I think, Doctor."

And, indeed, although most people would have simply registered the man's distinctive skin tone and the full moustache, with the hindsight of Holmes's observation, I could see nothing but Staunton's imperforate ear lobes.

All the contestants, save one, were on the field. Let battle commence!

It was certainly the strangest auction I have ever attended. To be frank, the objects offered for sale were a ragbag assortment at best and I remembered Holmes telling me that Mrs. Challenger had been particularly active in assembling them, often having to prise them from the Professor's reluctant grasp. Each one of them clearly had a sentimental value for him and the auction proceeded at a snail-like pace, as he wandered off into a discourse on each and every one of them.

As one lot gradually succeeded another, I became aware that—as with any auction—a separate theatre develops among the bidders and lead actors begin to emerge among the crowd.

There were two or three no nonsense men who were obviously dealers and who would have a well defined ceiling to what they were prepared to bid. There was a dusty academic who, I would have been prepared to wager, was bidding hopefully on behalf of a provincial museum and who looked well pleased to secure a couple of annotated maps.

There was an elderly spinster who was delighted with a pair of Challenger's old galoshes and who blushed crimson when he congratulated her on her excellent taste.

And then there was a rubicund middle aged man who, from his garb, was clearly American and almost certainly from somewhere in the West. Around his neck was slung what looked like a well-worn miner's knapsack. By contrast with the local bidders, who tended to signify their bids by a flick of their catalogues, he would raise his arm high to ensure he was noticed.

As lot succeeded lot, a pattern began to emerge. The dealers acquired most of what they came for and began to drift away. The amateur enthusiasts waved their catalogues until they had picked up their souvenir and then retired happy. The American seemed to bid enthusiastically on anything and everything but with a total lack of success and appeared increasingly frustrated.

Staunton bid on nothing but merely stood in his place by the wall, his catalogue tightly clenched in his hand and his eyes fixed unwaveringly on the podium where Challenger stood.

Finally, we came to Lot 21—an assortment of miscellaneous odds and ends.

Challenger picked up the items one at a time handling them lovingly. Here were the spectacles his father had worn on his first Amazon expedition, the occasion—he recalled as if it were yesterday—when he had narrowly escaped an attack of rabid piranha. Not for the first time in his rambling discourse I had a shrewd suspicion that much of the Professor's evident enjoyment was being derived by pulling the legs of his audience.

Now he had the familiar black leather book in his hands. He turned it over idly, as if it meant little to him.

"I'm afraid I can tell you little or nothing about this, ladies and gentlemen. I found it among my late father's effects. I believe the inscription may be in Sanskrit but I freely confess I have never wasted my time on dead languages. No, my interest has always been with hard evidence of the way people lived and shaped their world. Which is why my new expedition . . ."

And he was off on a word picture that threatened to take as long as the expedition itself.

It was at that point that a voice cut in.

"Ten pounds."

The voice was Staunton's and there was something in his tone that drew attention to him from those around him.

"Guineas!"

Now the American was bidding again. Staunton

looked surprised, then raised his bid to eleven pounds. Again the American cheerfully turned it into guineas.

"Twelve pounds." Staunton again.

"Fifty!"

There was a ripple of chatter around the room. Did this innocent American know what he was doing?

I saw a muscle tighten at the angle of Staunton's jaw.

"Guineas." And now he was smiling but without genuine amusement in the smile.

The room fell expectantly quiet, awaiting the American's response.

"One hundred . . . guineas."

Now Staunton's face was a picture of frustration. What was he to make of this madman? Then, it was as though his face had been wiped clean and an expression of pleased cunning began to form. The man decided on another course of action.

He made a grave little bow of concession in the direction of the American and put his catalogue in his pocket. Challenger rapped his gavel and the auction was over.

Now the journalists who had come along, largely in the hope of a display of Challenger histrionics, clustered around the American who seemed a little flustered by all this unexpected attention.

I indicated to Mycroft that we should move a little closer, so that we could eavesdrop on what was being said. Personally, I was beginning to feel like an actor in a play who has not been allowed to know the plot.

Surely *Staunton* was supposed to have acquired the Book of Kor?

Did this mean that Holmes's master plan had been aborted? And where *was* Holmes?

Now we could hear the journalists questioning the American. Who was he? Why did he want Challenger's castoffs so badly?

"No story in me, mah friends," he replied with a slight mid-western twang. "Diver's the name. Josiah H. Diver, Curator of the Museum of Human Life in Scottsdale, Arizona. 'Our Future is in Our Past'—that's our motto. We're not a big fancy institution like some I could name but we're mighty ambitious out there in Scottsdale, Arizona. Always admired the doings of the legendary Professor Challenger . . ."

Challenger would feast on this for days, I thought.

". . . and we figured that just about *anything* of his would be a real big attraction. So I just *had* to get that last lot of his. Or ah couldn't rightly go back home with mah head held high. Suppose I'm a sort of diplomat for the State of Arizona in mah own small way. Yes, sir, a diplomat . . ."

I turned to Mycroft, who was scanning the

room, which was slowly emptying. He shook his head to signify he had seen no sign of his brother. Challenger, too, had disappeared.

Now I noticed that Staunton had edged his way through the journalists and was whispering confidentially in Diver's ear. The American listened and was apparently intrigued by what he heard, for he nodded enthusiastically. He turned to make his apologies to the remaining journalists, then followed Staunton out of the Lounge.

I had the feeling that something significant had just happened in that room and that the significance had somehow eluded me. Something I had heard?

Whatever it was, the speculation was driven out of my mind by a hotel page boy, who appeared at my shoulder and offered me an envelope on a silver salver.

"Doctor Watson and Mr. Mycroft Holmes?"

"Yes, but . . ."

As I tentatively picked up the envelope, the page touched his forelock and was gone.

"Might it not be as well to read the contents, Doctor? Unless my eyes deceive me, the handwriting is my brother's."

I did as Mycroft suggested and in Holmes's precise hand I read—

"My Dear Watson and Mycroft—
On receipt of this note, I pray you make

your way immediately to the Zakhistan Consulate. You will find the garden gate open. On no account enter the house. Watch and listen and await the word of Kor. The game is almost over but the end game may be the most dangerous of all. And Watson—remember the deep waters!

HOLMES"

And then it came to me.

"We are divers in deep waters, Watson."

Of course—Josiah Diver of Scottsdale, Arizona was Holmes! And now Staunton had lured him—and the supposed Book of Kor—on to his own ground.

Or was it the other way around?

CHAPTER FIFTEEN

Challenger's auction had taken longer than I had realised, for it was nearly ten o'clock and fully dark when our cab dropped us at the entrance to Regent's Park nearest to the stretch of road that contained the embassies.

As I led the way I could not help but wonder what we should find. Holmes had called this the end game—but whose end was it to be? Staunton would stop at nothing now, for he had nothing to lose. What kind of plight did Uma find herself in? And precisely what role did Holmes expect *me* to play? So often in the past I had had to act on instinct. It was to be hoped that my instinct would not fail me on this most perilous occasion.

"Not that I am in the habit of frequenting London's public parks by night, but does it not strike you that an undue number of the local populace are abroad rather late, Doctor?"

And, indeed, now that Mycroft came to mention it, the road did seem a little busy for the time of night and the occupants were all men. Two or three were chatting, as if unwilling to call it a night; a few were strolling remarkably slowly and a couple seemed to be sweeping the street. That in itself was a sight I couldn't recall seeing at this time of night but perhaps it was one of the extra things the Regent's Park taxes paid for.

Then, as we passed the group of talkative friends, a voice said softly—

"Don't worry, Doctor—Mr. Mycroft—Lestrade here. We've got the place sealed up nice and tight. A worm couldn't wriggle out of there."

Yes, I thought, but how about a couple of snakes?

"Staunton went in just now—I recognised him right away, despite the boot polish. He had another feller with 'im. Just waiting for Mr. 'Olmes now."

You may have some time to wait, Lestrade, I said to myself.

A few paces further and we were at the garden gate of the Consulate. As Holmes had promised, it opened to the touch. Now we were in the garden with the gate pushed to behind us.

It was very much as I had described it to Holmes. The house itself was well set back from the road at the end of a row of formal flower beds but the main feature of the garden was a number of mature oak trees, still full of foliage, that would appear to have been planted when the house was first built. I was grateful for the shadows they cast, which enabled Mycroft and myself—neither of us particularly slight figures—to approach the house under their protective cover.

Immediately in front of us—just as Uma had described it to us—was the main reception room, which had a pair of French windows that opened out on to the garden. At the moment they were firmly closed and the curtains inside them drawn, allowing only a chink of light to fall on the flagstones outside.

What now?

As if he read my thoughts, Mycroft murmured in my ear—

"Remember Doctor—'Watch and wait and listen.' "

It was as if his words were a cue for, no sooner had he uttered them than the curtains were abruptly pulled back and one of the French windows opened a crack.

In the light that spilled out of the room I saw that Staunton was the person who had performed these acts. Luckily the contrast between the light of the room and the dark outside blinded him sufficiently to allow us to pull back out of his line of sight. As he turned back into the room, I heard Diver's unmistakable voice say—"Why, thank you kindly, sir . . ."

Holmes, I thought fleetingly, you really must be careful not to overdo this folksy accent.

". . . this asthma of mine can be real troublesome at this time of night. And it appears it doesn't take to that incense, or whatever it is, that you folks like so much. You see, the air in Scottsdale, Arizona, where I come from, is kind of dry . . ."

"As compared with the air in, say, Baker Street?"

I have often heard the phrase about someone's heart being in their mouth but I had never had the literal experience until that moment. I edged my way forward until I could just see into the room without revealing my own presence. What I saw did nothing to set my mind at rest.

Diver/Holmes was sitting in an armchair, his knapsack at his feet. Standing in front of him but at a safe distance, so that he could not be surprised by any sudden move on Holmes's part, was Staunton with a small revolver levelled at his heart.

"Oh, my dear Mr. Holmes, did you really think you could deceive me twice? How does the old saying go?

Fool me once—shame on you!
Fool me twice—shame on me!

"Your Pascal was a brilliant improvisation, I admit. But this stumbling simpleton was, frankly, beneath you. In fact, it causes me to wonder whether your remarkable reputation is all it is claimed to be.

"You know I intend to have the Book of Kor which, for all I knew, might have been lost years ago. You go to great pains to show me that it still exists, you create an occasion on which I can acquire it painlessly and *then* you have second thoughts. Is it because you and that dull doctor friend of yours. . . ."

Dull doctor!

". . . wish to gain favour with Madame Uma by returning it yourselves and making it seem that I have failed in my mission? In which case, I'm afraid it is you who have failed in yours."

I saw Holmes rise slowly to his feet. His whole bearing spoke of defeat. As he spoke he removed his false bushy eyebrows and pushed his hair back into place. With those simple gestures Diver was gone and Sherlock Holmes was back.

"I have clearly underestimated you, Staunton," he said and even his voice seemed weary. "You have been ahead of me at every turn. The death of Briggs was brilliant. Pelham's bold beyond belief. It took me far too long to see the scarlet thread of murder and where it led . . ."

But that's not true, I thought. Holmes picked it up from the very beginning. And then I realised why Mycroft and I had been instructed to wait and listen. Holmes was leading Staunton into a confession and we were to be the witnesses.

"Thank you, Mr. Holmes, I appreciate the compliment from one professional, as it were, to another. Yes, I can say I am modestly pleased with my efforts to date. The rest, I'm afraid—including, sadly, your dear brother—will have to wait for another occasion. But that day will come, never fear. Even though, equally sadly, you will not be here to witness it.

"When all this nonsense about Kor and the holy books crossed my path, I freely admit that my life was at a low ebb. But suddenly, everything fell into place, as if it were intended. That stupid book really did have power. If I used it properly, it would give me the excuse to wipe the slate clean. All those insults, all the humiliation—gone!

"Then, when I killed Briggs, the true inspiration came to me in a flash. The Sinners should die by their own hand, so to speak—by their own sins. After that it was a wonderful game to work out the variations. Pelham the Proud should die literally in the eyes of his peers. McKay the Pleasure Seeker in the throes of carnal lust. Pascal was to choke on his own creation. I was especially proud of that particular conceit but you spoiled it all with your meddling, Mr. Sherlock Holmes.

"Your sin should be 'A' for Arrogance, my friend. Did you really think that you could walk into my parlour and prevail?"

"Clearly, I was mistaken. So what is *my* fate to be?"

"I believe you deserve the highest accolade of all, Mr. Holmes. Let us return to the font of all wisdom in this of all places. You shall receive the Kiss of Kor . . ."

Still covering Holmes with his revolver, Staunton backed slowly towards the mantelpiece. Beside it hung a tasselled cord. When his hand encountered it, he tugged it viciously. Deep in the recesses of the house I heard a bell peal.

From my pocket I pulled my service revolver and cocked it as quietly as possible. I felt sure Holmes would want me to wait until he gave me a sign but of one thing I was sure. That devil Staunton was not leaving this room alive, if John H. Watson had any say in the matter.

And then it was as if I were watching some Lyceum melodrama from a box. Double doors at the end of the room swung inwards and into the room swept Uma, the Emerald Lady, followed by Khali, carrying a large basket embroidered with the insignia of Kor, which he set carefully on the ground and stepped back.

I could not take my eyes off Uma. Her raiment—for one could hardly call it mere clothing—was a brilliant emerald green from the jewelled combs that held her upswept hair to the cloak that touched the floor. All that could be seen of her was the impassive mask of her face and the delicate hands emerging from her long sleeves and they, too, were decorated with emerald rings and bracelets.

The woman glittered—all except for her eyes. From where I stood they seemed totally dead.

Had Staunton drugged her in some way to keep her under his control?

I turned towards Mycroft. Was it time to intervene? But a firm shake of the head confirmed my own feeling that the drama must play out a little further. Now both Holmes and Uma were at risk.

With his "cast" in place, Staunton looked positively smug. Turning towards Uma, he addressed her in what I presumed to be the manner he had chosen to indicate deference to her position.

"Your Highness, I have brought before you, as I promised, the infidel who possesses the holy Book of Kor. May it please you to reveal to him the twin Guardians of Kor's will?"

Still seeming to be in some sort of trance, Uma turned her head slightly in Staunton's direction.

"You have done well, friend Smith, and it was well you did, for the Guardians were beginning to be angry and their anger is to be feared."

Then, abruptly, she clapped her hands once. Khali sprang forward and removed the lid of the basket before stepping smartly back.

Then my blood froze and I distinctly felt Mycroft beside me shudder, too. For from the basket in perfect synchronisation rose two of the largest snakes I had ever seen in my life.

They were King Cobras and fully four feet in length. Around their hideous heads their distinctive hoods were fully extended, so that they appeared to be two evil spirits peering out from beneath a rock. Even more disturbing was the way those heads were in constant motion, as though they were scanning the room in search of their prey.

Now Uma approached the basket and, as she did so, she seemed to be chanting in some strange tongue. Whatever it was, the twin serpents clearly found it comforting, for they fixed their gaze solely on their mistress.

Then I could scarcely credit what I was seeing, as she reached into the basket and picked up a snake in each hand and held them aloft. As a feat of strength alone it was something to be wondered at, for these were no ordinary creatures. As a spectacle it was both rivetting and horrifying and will be with me to my dying day. Uma stood there like some glorious pagan goddess—which, in a sense, of course, she was.

Staunton moved closer to Holmes and pointed with his revolver to the knapsack at Holmes's feet.

"And now, if you please, the Book of Kor."

If I did not know that my friend must have some trick up his sleeve, I should have said that he presented the very picture of defeat, as he slowly reached down and unfastened the strap.

"Careful, Mr. Holmes—just the Book."

Holmes reached inside the knapsack and

brought out the by now all-too-familiar black leather volume.

"Take the cursed thing, Staunton, and be done with it," he said and tossed it casually in the man's direction. As he did so, even from where I stood, I thought I caught a faint gleam in those deep set eyes.

Staunton deftly caught the book one-handed, never taking his eyes off his adversary. Once he held it in his hand, a smile of utter triumph lit up that bland face.

Then, as he thumbed through it, it vanished as suddenly as it had come, to be replaced by an expression of terrible fury. It was as though another person altogether had suddenly inhabited his body.

"But *this* is not the Book of Kor!" he hissed.

It was a different Holmes who answered him.

"It is *a* Book of Kor. I do not think anyone ever promised that it was *the* Book of Kor. However, you may find the contents to be of more practical value. I believe they are derived from *Mrs. Fernworthy's Book of Botany for Beginners*— an excellent treatise on the subject, so I am told."

I had heard of people being "possessed" and now I saw it with my own eyes. All the frustration and failure in Staunton's life seemed compressed into that one moment of public humiliation. His eyes blazed fire at the man who had brought him to this pass and the hand with the revolver slowly began to rise towards Holmes.

At which moment Holmes said one word in a calm, distinct voice.

"Kor!"

And then things happened in such a blur that, even now, I have trouble sorting out the exact sequence in my mind.

The statue that was Uma suddenly came to life.

With a sudden dramatic gesture her arms were flung wide as she threw the twin serpents at Staunton and Khali. In her grasp they had been strangely somnolent. Now this rude shock enraged them. Each of them entwined itself around its new and reluctant host, their heads moved back in concert and—faster than the eye could see—they sank their fangs into their victim's necks.

In the same instant the two men screamed as one—a high pitched scream that told of indescribable pain. Staunton's revolver fell from his hand and slid across the polished wood floor, where Holmes bent down to reach for it.

I saw Uma shake her head, as if she were waking from a nightmare. Then her eyes widened with shock, as she saw the two bodies writhing on the ground. And perhaps with something else.

The twin serpents had wreaked their vengeance but their anger remained unabated.

While Holmes was busy retrieving Staunton's

revolver, he was unable to see what Uma and I could observe all too well. The serpents were in the process of unwinding themselves from their initial prey.

Those malevolent heads rose and pivotted to scan the room in search of new targets. First they looked at their mistress and I had the distinct impression that they were questioning her about the way she had treated them. But then their lifelong training seemed to hold sway and, as one, they turned to the only other living being in that room of death.

Sherlock Holmes.

With awful majesty they moved in his direction and it was then that I remembered something I had read in the entry in Holmes's Index.

The King Cobra retains enough poison after its first strike to allow it a second. Holmes was doomed unless . . .

It was the work of a second to step through the open window, point my service revolver and fire. The head of the cobra on the right exploded before my eyes.

But even as I fired, I heard what I assumed was an echo and then—the second cobra suffered the same fate as the first.

"Well done, Watson! You're beginning to make a habit of saving my life, old fellow." Holmes was at my side and reaching out to take my hand and Mycroft's in each of his own. "And now you might take care of a very gallant lady—in your professional capacity, of course."

And, indeed, Uma looked about to faint, as I helped her to a chair.

"Is it over, John?"

"Yes, my dear," I reassured her, "it's all over."

Then, as sobs shook her body, I placed my arm around her shoulder. It seemed the appropriate thing to do.

Behind me I was aware of other people entering the room and a familiar voice boomed—

"Remarkable rifle, the Lee Enfield. Don't know when I last had a chance at a shot like that. Mombassa, perhaps. Wait until Summerlee hears about this! Of course, the old fool will say I would have done better with a Webley . . ."

So, it was Challenger who had fired that second shot?

As I turned in his direction, he was smiling triumphantly and stroking his beard.

"That's right, Doctor, I was perched in that oak tree just outside the window. A second line of defence, you might say, covering your back. But when I saw the mood those cobras were in, I couldn't be sure you'd have time for a second shot. Perhaps we should take our sharp-shooting act on the music hall stage. I can see it now . . ." he sketched the imaginary billing in the air with his hands—". . . 'CHALLENGER & Watson!' " I could just see the comparative size of our names.

245

"Over here, gentlemen, and please hurry."

It was Mycroft, who was kneeling over Staunton. As we joined him, it was obvious that, though Staunton was still barely alive, he was sinking fast. His eyes were flickering but he seemed to recognise Mycroft at least.

Then, painfully, he spoke. We had to lean close to hear his words.

"Glad it's over at last . . . Perhaps these people are right about a second life . . . soon know . . . Try to do better next time . . ."

Then the eyes glazed over. I reached past Mycroft and performed that function that transcends time and culture. I closed his eyelids.

And in that room of death we all instinctively bowed our heads in a moment of silence for *all* the departed.

CHAPTER SIXTEEN

It was two weeks or so later and the weather had turned unseasonably cold—to the point where Mrs. Hudson, without being asked, had lit a fire in our sitting room. Outside the gas lamps were just beginning to win their daily battle with the fading sun and a sharp wind gave notice of harsh days to come.

Lestrade had just left after briefing us on the aftermath to that evening of horror at the Consulate.

"After due consideration and consultation with Mr. Mycroft Holmes 'ere, representing the 'Ome Office of Her Majesty's Government . . ."

Mycroft's face might have been carved from stone and I had an idiotic vision of him on a pedestal in Pall Mall, somewhere near the Diogenes Club, with the legend—THE UNKNOWN DIPLOMAT.

Lestrade continued in his best official tones—

". . . the official record will show that two dangerous snakes escaped from Regent's Park Zoo, found their way into the Zakhistan Consulate and were the cause of the tragic death of two of the diplomats in residence. Fortunately, the coincidental presence in the neighbourhood of a contingent of police officers engaged in a training exercise . . ."

"Ably led by Inspector Lestrade of Scotland Yard," Holmes interposed but the Inspector chose to ignore him.

". . . was able to contain the situation . . ."

"Through the use of a Lee Enfield rifle, which they just happened to have in their possession." Now it was Challenger's turn.

"And what about the deaths of the three Sinners?" I asked, putting an end to what promised to turn into frivolity.

It was Mycroft who answered me.

"They will remain technically 'open files' of unsolved murders. The police have reason to believe that they were the work of a single individual who is no longer in this country. Investigations will continue."

Then, seeing my expression, he continued—

"An unsatisfactory conclusion, I know, Doctor, but frankly, there would be nothing to be gained by dragging this through the public courts. You can hardly punish a dead man twice."

"And what of Uma?" I persisted.

"I think I can answer that." Holmes rose from his armchair and began to pace the room, coming to rest behind the chair in which she was sitting wearing the green dress in which I had first seen her.

"Since nothing illegal apparently happened in that house that night, there can, by definition, be no criminal charges. And since I suspect that the Zakhistan Consulate may shortly be relocating its personnel . . ."

I looked enquiringly at the Emerald Lady— as I shall always think of her—and she nodded almost imperceptibly.

"Forgive me for contradicting you, Mr. Holmes—for I and my people are eternally in your debt—but something *did* happen in that room that night that I cannot explain.

"I got your note, of course . . ."

That explained the second note, I thought.

". . . and I knew precisely what would happen and what I had to do. Staunton was suspicious, that I could see, but I burned it as soon as I had read it. As I waited for the summons, I was quite calm. And then, suddenly, the strangest feeling began to steal over me. I *was* the High Priestess of Kor. I was the incarnation of *all* the High Priestesses who had preceded me or would follow me. It was as though my destiny had led me to this one moment.

"When I had the holy serpents in my hands, it was as though I was possessed by a force greater than myself. Someone seemed to speak to me. I heard no words but the message was clear. It told me that the traitors must be punished and I must be the means. I am sorry for Khali but the man you call Staunton had subverted him beyond recall . . ."

"This 'force' you speak of?" I interjected.

"You will think me foolish, gentlemen, but I could swear it was the voice of Kor—and something about it told me it was the last time I or any of us should ever hear it. Kor's time with us is over. It is for us to make our way in this new world. I must return to my people one last time to tell them so and point the path."

By the time she had finished speaking her eyes were bright. As High Priestess or as some other kind of leader, her people were, indeed fortunate.

Out of the ensuing silence a quiet voice said—

"Madam, I would like you to have this in your own keeping. Personally, I detest people who borrow books and do not return them. It comes with the sincere regard of George Edward Challenger."

Then Challenger crossed the room and proffered that familiar worn black book. The genuine Book of Kor.

Uma took it and ran her fingers over the raised lettering. She seemed to be speaking to the object in her hands as she said—

"Whoever you were, you came to us from the elements. For so long you gave us a purpose and made us a people. But now it is up to us to make our own destiny. And Kor is free to return to the elements . . ."

And with a movement of her arm that brought all too readily to mind her gesture of the other night, she threw the Book of Kor into the fire.

All of us were so taken aback by what she had done that we watched mutely as the flames slowly licked at the pages, found them good and began to devour them. Perhaps there was something in the ancient ink but it seemed as if the flames began to sparkle and hiss and, if I were a superstitious man, I could swear that I saw visions in them, coming and going, as they vanished up that familiar chimney.

Every face in that room was turned in that one direction and, as the glow from the fire slowly faded from their faces, there was a collective sigh, as of relief.

Then Uma rose to her feet. For a moment she was a queen surveying her subjects.

"Mr. Holmes—John—I can never thank you properly, so I will not even try. When I asked you earlier about your fee, I remember you told me that you never vary it, except when you remit it entirely . . ."

"Which in this case I most certainly do," Holmes replied gravely.

"But you cannot refuse me the right to bestow on you both the High Order of Kor . . ."

And she reached into her purse and produced two green leather purses fastened with silk cords, which she handed to each of us. I tipped out the contents and there, gleaming on my palm, were two cufflinks set with emeralds. Holmes, I could see, had received the same.

She smiled a little sadly.

"I must admit that I have just invented that Order but I hope that it will mean that every now and then you will remember the Emerald Lady. And who knows—perhaps we may all meet again?"

A moment later, as we all stood, she had left the room.

With her departure we seemed to have said all there was to say. The only further surprise was that Challenger managed to bully Mycroft into accompanying him to the Explorers' Club for dinner, where I could imagine the other members were due to be regaled with exaggerated stories of how he, George Edward Challenger, had single-handedly exterminated a veritable nest of serpents, thus saving the civilised world.

Then Holmes and I were left alone in that companionable silence that followed an adventure.

I don't know what was going through that complex mind but mine was full of a jumble of impressions from these last eventful days . . . Challenger's booming voice . . . the sorcery of Holmes's hands as he concocted Pascal's *Surprise* . . . the revelation dawning in the eyes of the dying Staunton and the pity in Mycroft's—

and most of all, the mesmerising presence of Uma.

"You're quite right, Watson, it *will* make an excellent narrative in your collection one of these days but not just yet, I fear. Oh, don't look so surprised. When a man fingers the cufflinks he has just been given, looks immediately at the bureau where his writing implements are kept, then flexes the fingers of his right hand, as though he held a pen in it, it is not difficult to see the old literary warhorse champing at the bit.

"But there are too many people who would be hurt by such an account at this time, old fellow, not least the lady herself. We shall hear more of her in years to come, I fancy. The day will come when women of her mettle will lead nations but perhaps not in our time, Watson, perhaps not in our time."

"Promise me one thing, Holmes," I said to change the subject. "No more cases involving snakes, if you don't mind. I had enough of them with that 'Speckled Band' affair but this was . . ."

"Monstrous?" And he laughed his distinctive silent laugh.

Then he became serious once more.

"But you know, there is a distinct pattern in life's carpet and things repeat themselves endlessly—predictably even, if one can determine the pattern. The people we have been involved with found themselves on a particular point in the pattern when they were at Oxford. Each of them went his separate way—only to find himself back at what looked like an identical spot in the pattern.

"I venture to suggest that those who are left will have learned a lesson from the experience that will last them the rest of their lives."

"And other people, too, I would hope?"

"Ah, there's the rub, old fellow. Even as we sit here, there are people in Oxford or Rangoon, Chicago, Peking, you name it, committing acts in all innocence that will come back to haunt them who knows when?"

"Whenever the pattern in the carpet recurs?"

"Just so, I'm afraid. And now, my dear fellow, I intend to defy the gods and commit a small sin of my own . . ."

"And that is?"

"If you will be so good as to pass me my Stradivarius, which is by your elbow, I shall play you a new composition of my own invention. I call it 'Sonata for Sinners.' At the very least it may act as a form of exorcism!"

Books are produced
in the United States
using U.S.-based
materials

Books are printed
using a revolutionary
new process called
THINKtech™ that
lowers energy usage
by 70% and increases
overall quality

Books are durable
and flexible because
of smythe-sewing

Paper is sourced
using environmentally
responsible foresting
methods and the
paper is acid-free

Center Point Large Print
600 Brooks Road / PO Box 1
Thorndike, ME 04986-0001 USA

(207) 568-3717

US & Canada:
1 800 929-9108
www.centerpointlargeprint.com